A Hero's Calling

Wind of Destiny, Volume One

AJ Cooper

SANCTON
THE BLESSED ISLES
Eloesus
RIVER SULIS
PALLISTRIX
ISTEROS
ARCTOS
AGATHE
TIGRIS
IOGHEIRA
THÉNAI
THENOA
STRAITEIRA
KERSEPOLI
KERSICA
KORTHOS
KORTHICA
TEN CITIES
THARTA
THARTICA
ARKADIOS
THEMURIA
100 mi.   200 mi.   300 mi.   400 mi.   500 mi.

THE GATHERING

The word went out from Seshán and that word was law.

From the northern hills to the burning plains, from the lowland jungles to the high mountain passes, the padisha emperor's command was clear: "Mobilize."

The Great Lords of Fharas gathered their warriors and the kings and queens in the tropical seas called upon their vassals. The army would shake the foundations of the earth. No force like it had ever been seen before, nor would its like ever be seen again. A monstrous human horde, a million strong, would soon gobble up the countryside and march north to "bring the goatherds of Eloesus into the empire's fold."

THE WANDERER

The priestess sought Phillipidēs
"Phillipidēs!" she cried and said,
"What do you seek above all things?
Above all gems and gold and pow'r?"
Then answered brave Phillipidēs,
"I seek one thing above all else:
Fame imperishable and true,
A name exalted for all time."

—Arkelaios

THÉNAI

The sun beat hot on the market square of Thénai, sapping the will and energy of those unlucky enough to stand in its path. A haze had formed like smoke, drifting up into the cloudless blue sky. Merchants cowered underneath their stalls. Every person able to stay inside did so—everyone except Theron.

Theron stood there, braving the heat, wearing no shirt to guard his sunburnt skin. There was trouble in Theron's beloved city… a thief. Someone had stolen an item of great value—specifically, a cloak of black Hymnian wool. Though hundreds of thousands of souls lived in the city of Thénai—the place he called his community, his home—Theron was determined to uncover the wrongdoer. A black Hymnian cloak was worth more money than many would see in their lifetimes. He had won it in war; it was a piece of loot he had been allowed to keep. He had earned it—and he would not lose it.

He eyed the people gathered in the market square. There was a man selling perfumes and oils from the Far South; a woman hawking purple tunics from Khazidea; a dusky Kheroan offering caged monkeys and green parrots. There was even an amazon, standing there in leathers and pretending not to care about the heat, guarding the variety of swords, axes, and throwing knives she had for sale.

None had the black Hymnian cloak—or so it appeared. Things were very rarely as they appeared, Theron knew. He had answered the call of his community and gone to war—he had armed himself with spear and shield and worn the bronze breastplate of a hoplite. He had fought the vicious, warlike city of Kersepoli which had long sought to dominate Thénai. He had raided a house to find a young girl, scared to death, and tried to reassure her—yet she had a dagger hidden behind her back. The killing of that girl had been the hardest of the campaign.

So often people hid their darker natures. Any one of these merchants could be hiding the cloak.

On a road lined with palm trees Theron eyed the people walking by. Few were hardy enough to brave the midday sun. There were hoplites on guard as well as a handful of young men and women. Some, no doubt, were headed to the theater. Theron's friend Phaido was performing there. Phaido, an actor, a singer, a dancer, and a piper, just barely scraped by. His performances at the theater only earned him a silver or two a night. He never drew a large enough crowd to fill the seats.

Theron crossed down another road, also lined with palms, where many red-roofed houses lay. This street was paved with white stone, a wonder in a city of mostly dirt roads. Anyone lucky to live here was far too good to associate with Theron. And yet the homes of the rich often hid secrets too. Many were not content with their riches—some, perhaps, were discontent enough to steal a black Hymnian cloak.

The midday sun had begun to wane, and many streets had been explored, when it dawned on Theron that he had wasted a day. The black Hymnian cloak was lost and he would never recover it. No doubt the thief had grabbed it from his house and then fled the city altogether, never to be seen again. Alas for that rich black hue, as dark as the space between the stars. Alas for that embroidery in gold thread, and the red ruby which clasped it together. *I will never see you again, Black Hymnian Cloak. Farewell!*

It was near night when Theron's wandering took him to the theater. The stone edifice had been dedicated not so long ago in a grand ceremony. Brecko, lord of drama and performance, had been honored with a dozen sacrifices—white bulls from the coast, goats from the highlands and sheep from the outlying pastures. Carvings of Brecko and his favored animal, the panther, decorated the building, which was lined with marble columns and entered via a long white colonnade.

When he entered the theater, having paid his silver coin, it was as he expected—the crowd was not large enough to fill even half the seats, and the people were sitting far apart. It was one of Phaido's most disastrous performances yet.

But Phaido stood there on the stage confidently—wearing Theron's black Hymnian cloak.

Theron shot up out of his seat. Wild, hot fury coursed through his veins. This could not be. It simply couldn't!

He wanted to wrap his arms around Phaido's neck, squeeze until his head turned blue. He would show that singing, dancing buffoon how a man of war dealt with his problems. He would spear him straight through, impale him like meat on a stick, cut off his head with his shortsword.

Then Theron sat down to catch his breath and, for some reason, began to laugh.

He laughed more and more as Phaido recited his lines.

"We Eloesians are scattered across the sea like frogs around a pond..."

Theron would have his cloak after all—once he wrung it from Phaido's body and delivered a solid punch.

"We are far apart and yet close!" Phaido continued. "Close, and yet divided. We have settled over all the world and founded cities to glorify the nation's name. Though wars will be fought until the end of our history, let us never forget that we are of one blood..."

Phaido had finally got him. Theron wiped tears of laughter

from his eyes. No doubt, he looked like a madman.

"Let those who defame the Eloesian name know they are fools, the sons of serpents!" cried Phaido.

He was straying from the lines, but he had gotten the audience's attention.

"Let the Fharese and all the heathen south know that they are less than we!" snapped Phaido, sensing that after all these hours he had gotten the crowd's attention. "Let the Fharese tyrant emperor fall! The glory of the Old Dominion is not in him! The Fharese emperor wishes to make slaves of all men—I say, a pox on his head! He will not succeed, by Brecko's beard!"

The crowd began to cheer. For once, Phaido had succeeded in rousing someone besides himself. Theron was proud of his friend—proud, but still a bit angered by the cloak.

"We are more than frogs around a pond!" Phaido finished. "We are lizards—no, crocodiles of the Khazan! We will always be free!" He took a bow and the crowd stood up in applause—all except one, a government official judging by his white chiton and blue sash. Perhaps the archon, Epaphras, had sent him to keep an eye on the theater.

Theron stood up and applauded as well. That solid punch would come later.

~

Theron met Phaido outside the theater. The waning sunlight reflected harshly on his curly golden hair. His dark eyes had a happiness and joy that Theron had not seen in ages. Some of that was no doubt due to the successful performance—but most was due to his successful heist, that cloak of black Hymnian wool.

"You deserve a punch," said Theron, "but I can't do it. I have not seen such a big smile from you in years."

"No, you haven't," said Phaido. He burst into laughter as he undid the cloak's clasp. "I was wondering how long it would take you to find it."

Theron smiled. "I wonder how wealthy you will get from this performance."

"Wealthy enough to buy a bottle of wine," said Phaido, "or a hunk of cheese."

Theron laughed as he fixed the cloak around his neck. "To the tavern?"

"Yes!" said Phaido. "To the tavern we go!"

Theron woke up in the early morning light in his rented room. Below his floor, the shoemaker had already begun his day's work and was cursing up a storm. Phaido slept on the floor with only a tattered blanket to cover him. He had no memories of last night—a sign of a good time, no doubt.

Someone was pounding on the door—the only reason he had awoken this early. He hurried out of bed and threw on his tunic. Groggily he answered, opening the door to find a man in a chiton and a blue sash. Theron's heart leapt in his chest at the sight. This could only be bad news.

"I am here on behalf of His Excellency the archon of Thénai," said the man in the chiton.

"The archon?" said Theron. "Epaphras? Who are you?"

Phaido awoke behind him, cursing.

"Names are not important," said the man in the chiton. "I am a politarch—the Politarch of Public Order, no less. I understand you are hiding a certain rascal by the name of Phaido. Both you and he are summoned to court immediately. Come with me!"

"What is the meaning of this?" cried Phaido. "What are the charges?"

"Disturbing the peace!" answered the censor.

Theron cursed, refusing to believe all this was taking place. What charges could possibly be brought against them? He had committed no crime, nor had Phaido. Still he had no chance against the city officials and the Thenoan soldiers who backed them. He hurriedly donned his trousers and sandals and draped the black Hymnian cloak over his neck. He left with the politarch and Phaido was only a step behind.

~

In the rosy light of dawn, Theron and Phaido were led from the room through Thénai's winding, dusty streets through the market square and finally up a grueling set of stone steps to the High City. There the priests of Amara the War Maiden, patron goddess of Thénai, had their temple. In the shade of its towering pillars were the law courts where the archon presided. Still, Theron could not believe what was happening—to be treated as a criminal for allowing Phaido to sleep in his house… Phaido, who had done nothing wrong, only given a poor performance of a famous monologue. If bad acting was a crime, Phaido would have been force-fed a bowl of hemlock many years ago.

The archon was waiting for him after they had finished the exhausting climb. Below them, the red roofs of the city buildings stretched into the distance. The people of Thénai were just waking up—and yet Theron was here, treated as lower than scum, a common criminal on par with a murderer or a black theurge.

The trial had all the markings of a criminal proceeding. The archon Epaphras sat on a high seat, his hair a light shade of gray. His dark eyes were condemning, judgmental. On either side of him were statues: the goddess Justice, holding scales in her hands, and the god Mercy, offering an empty platter.

Theron still could not quite believe what was happening. As far as he knew he had done nothing wrong. Nor had Phaido. Perhaps they had committed some horrid act in their wine-fueled debauch. Stranger things had happened, no doubt. "What are our charges?" he asked as he was forced within ten feet of Epaphras' seat. He fell to his knees and Phaido followed.

"Disturbing the peace—for Phaido," said Epaphras. "For you, aiding him."

What *had* happened last night? "If we did something, I cannot remember… the wine…"

"Wine had nothing to do with it," said Epaphras. "Your friend committed his deed while very serious and sober. He spoke out against the Fharese. He defamed the padisha emperor. His thoughtless words may cost Eloesus its freedom."

Theron scoffed. The padisha emperor was hundreds of miles away, in a land—the Southern World—far out of sight and far out of mind. Though his eyes were everywhere, and each listening ear might belong to a spy, surely he would not start a war because of Phaido—because of a poor, pitiful actor in a city of no real consequence.

"I thought we Thenoans loved liberty," said Phaido. "I thought we considered death better than slavery…"

"Watch your words," said Epaphras. "Whip him!"

Theron had been so focused on Epaphras he had neglected the hoplites lining the square. Within seconds the thongs had cracked, splitting open Phaido's back. Tears formed in Theron's eyes.

"The King of Kings could destroy all Eloesus if he set his mind to it," Epaphras said. "How would you like to see the pastures of Thenoa in flame… to see the mountain shrines turned to rubble, the cities razed to ashes, the people sold into bondage…"

Theron cursed. In an instant a whip struck him, tearing

through his skin and opening up a raw, tender wound. New tears formed in his eyes, tears of pain, of pity for himself.

"Do you admit you spoke against him, Phaido? Do you admit you defamed the Fharese?" Epaphras said.

"Of course," Phaido said. The pain in his voice was evident. Streams of red were dripping down his back, collecting on the stone-paved ground.

"Theron," said Epaphras, "you are a man of good standing, a veteran of high worth. The community will never forget your bravery in the Kersepolan War. You I sentence to a small fine… ten *doukon*."

Ten *doukon* was still more than Theron had, a week's worth of wages for a typical laborer. He had two, maybe three *doukon* to his name. He would have to sell his precious cloak.

"But you, rabble rouser," sneered Epaphras, his scorn dripping through his words. "Your idle talk and dangerous boasting has cost you your life. I set your life price at one-hundred *doukon*, payable by sundown. Else, you will have to drink deep of hemlock."

"A curse on you!" cried Theron. He unclasped his cloak and tossed it on the ground. "This is of Hymnian wool, embroidered in thread. It is worth ten times its weight in gold. I give you that—for Phaido's life, and mine."

"Bring it to me," said Epaphras. A hoplite speared it and lifted it to him, like a fish caught in a net. Epaphras stroked it with his old, wrinkled hands. "Fine make. It probably cost you your life's savings. A pity it will be mine now."

"A pity," Theron repeated, but he cared no longer. There were things more important than a black Hymnian cloak… Phaido's life, and his.

"This embroidery is of an old pattern," said Epaphras, for a moment apparently forgetting where he was, focusing all his attention on the cloak. His dark eyes scanned the length of the black wool and the abstract patterns laced in gold around its edge. "Your life price is paid." Epaphras met Theron's gaze. "So is your fine… Phaido, you are exiled forever from Thénai. Your home and your possessions belong to the city, now… to me."

"If he is exiled," said Theron, "then so am I." He turned to his friend Phaido, saw tears glistening in his eyes. All that he had—his home, his hope, the city he had loved—were taken from him. In a way banishment was worse than death. If they were no longer Thenoans, what indeed were they? Vagrants, city-less wanderers. Not even the goatherds or the mountain folk would accept them. They belonged nowhere, now. The wild woods and desert barrens were now their home. They would hunger and seek rest but find no food nor shelter. Only the gods could help them now—and the gods were dead.

What am I, if not a Thenoan?

"Thénai does not need folk like you," said Epaphras. "Your dangerous words could yet draw the padisha emperor's ire. The community is better without you. I forbid you from saying farewell to your neighbors. All your possessions will remain here. Lead them out, soldiers!"

His heart sunken, Theron descended from the High City. Phaido followed, even more grudgingly than he.

THENOA

What lay outside the city walls? Phaido had taken in the pastoral sights before, but they seemed different now.

The hills surrounding the city Phaido had loved were covered in sheep and goats—little spots of white and brown on a gold canvas. In some places, there were olive groves. The country folk grew all the food and sheared all the wool, but the city dwellers despised them nonetheless. It was true, the country folk were ignorant—ignorant of democracy, of government, of geography and the arts. Yet they lived in what the poet Dioscouros claimed to long for—the pastoral ideal, the life in the country free from the cares of civilization. Would Phaido now break his back in the iron mines, he wondered as he eyed the distant mountain peaks. He was not fit for work. But in truth he was not fit for acting or singing either. He had failed for so long without giving up, it had become a flaw in his character. At the thought a jab of despair took him in his heart.

The road stretched before him, a wide dirt path that wound its way through the hills before disappearing into the distance. That road would take him to Kersepoli and the other three great cities of the Eloesian coast. Yet he did not belong there. He would be rejected out of hand, an outsider, a stranger. When they saw him they would know his nature—exile. He was lower than dirt, of less value than the brown earth of the road.

"Where to?" said Theron. "To Kersica?"

Phaido laughed, though he had no time for humor. "I do not want to be taken slave." The Kersepolans would enslave free Eloesians without a moment's thought and add to their ever-growing underclass. "Let's walk," he said. The road would take them somewhere, somehow.

It was late at night and they were far from the city, further than they had ever been. The stars had never shone so bright. The earth had grown barren and rocky. A cold breeze was blowing off the nearby mountains. Civilization had disappeared behind them. It seemed that here, not even shepherds led their flocks.

A dark figure appeared in the distance. Phaido gasped and grabbed Theron, the only one armed. Theron grabbed his spear and readied it.

More figures appeared. They were grunting and hawing. One approached tentatively—by the light of Phaido's torch he could see thick brown fur and a wild mane of hair, a short, squat build and crazed yellow eyes. It half-walked, half-crawled on all fours, never letting one hand off the ground.

Phaido could barely breath for fear. Its eyes reflected in the fire—yellow like putrid water, crazed and hungry. Its mouth and forehead were hairless, revealing tawny skin. Phaido had never seen anything like this before, nor heard of it—not in life, not in any idle myths.

Theron jabbed his spear but the creature bucked away and shrieked. At its shriek its fellow beasts called out in loud, shrill voices. Phaido had never seen such a monstrosity. His entire body was shaking. The night air had never felt so cold. He realized that, despite being exiled, despite losing the city and the community he had loved, he did not want to die. He wanted nothing more than life.

A rock struck the crazed creature in the head. It staggered backward and fell to the rocky ground. Then it bucked up, jabbering, and fled away. Its fellow beasts followed in a stampede. They were gone. But something had thrown that rock—something more dangerous than the monsters themselves.

THE FOOTHILLS OF UPPER THENOA

They were being followed. That much was apparent, but Theron did not want to frighten his friend. These monstrous creatures—whatever they were—had the look of hunger in their eyes. Theron had no chance against all those dozens of them. But whatever followed Theron and Phaido—whatever had hurled that giant rock—had scared the creatures off utterly. There were cyclops in the islands of the Middle Sea… could one have swam ashore? There were cyclops in Wild Themuria, too… had one climbed down this far, hungry for Theron and Phaido's flesh?

No, something darker and more terrible than a cyclops was following them. Something out of nightmares that stalked mankind, not wanting to share his flesh with beasts. "We have to rest," said Theron.

Phaido nodded his agreement but Theron could read the terror written in his expression. He was pale and his eyes were wide and glazed. He had no arguments against Theron's suggestion. Mankind needed to sleep—even if the monster stalking them did not.

Phaido looked around, searching the darkness for whatever had thrown that giant rock.

"It was probably the wind," said Theron. "We are near the mountains. There are strong gusts."

"Indeed," Phaido said and eyed the ground. He undid his pack and rolled out his sleeping mat.

There was no gust that blew that rock. Such a gust would have knocked both Theron and Phaido down. It had been thrown. As Phaido got settled, Theron said, "I'm going to have a look around." He left his friend in the dark, a bit guilty but intensely curious—curious, and worried.

In the dim light, Theron could see no creature stirring. The dim glow of the moon was masked by clouds. Chirping echoed through the mountain hollows, through the shrub pines and the bare hills. The air smelled somehow fresher. But danger lurked nearby, close enough to strike, close enough to kill. Of that Theron was sure. Something out of nightmares hid among these mountains. But he could do nothing about it.

He turned and left amid the chirping of the night. The land looked empty, giving no hint of what danger lurked within.

~

The sun arose, banishing the fear of the night and waking Theron. He had stayed up late, intending not to sleep, but eventually the fatigue of travel had worn him down. He had expected all that time for the nightmare to emerge from the shadows—the monster with the rock who had scared away their attackers, no doubt ten times as fearsome as they.

The sky had a rosy hue in the dawn's light. The mountain peaks towered above them, clearly visible, appearing deceptively close. It would take many days to reach the top of those snowcapped peaks.

Below, down a deep valley, was Thenoa proper. The pastures and goatherds had passed them by. Now in the barren foothills, a region of rocks and dry earth, no life stirred. In places there were pools of water and fresh springs, but no wealth to be had—no iron or timber, hardly any grass, only barren earth and shrub pines. He scanned the area, seeing no sign of the crazed beasts or the creature which had thrown the rock.

The sky was bright and cloudless as Phaido stirred awake. Vast regions lay all around them and still Theron did not know where he was headed. No village would accept them as their own— each man belonged to his own city, to his own home. Exiles were as low as dirt—worse than slaves, worse than criminals, worse than barbarians. Even the blond, blue-eyed warriors of the far north were better in Eloesians' eyes.

"What is left for us?" said Phaido, unusually keen for such an early hour. "Is a life of crime our only option?"

"We could leave Thenoa," said Theron. "You could perform across the land…" But Phaido's skills were less than exemplary. His acting was stiff, his voice strained, his fingers on the lyre passionless.

Phaido laughed. "Ah, yes… I can just imagine, Phaido Treibanos, who can barely fill a dozen seats in Thénai's theater, drawing crowds in other cities…"

Theron sighed. He was out of ideas. And they were in danger—danger that was keenly felt, evident in Phaido's tone. There were monsters nearby, stalking them. "We need to find safe shelter," said Theron. Perhaps they could pledge themselves as bondservants—even sell themselves into slavery. A city's walls would protect them—losing their freedom was a small price to pay for precious life.

Phaido was scanning the barren hills, looking for signs of their attackers perhaps. There were no tawny-furred beasts, however, lurking amid the scrub brush. "We shouldn't stay here long… this road must lead somewhere, hmmm? I hope it is not taking us to Kersica…"

Slavery in Korthos or Tharta was one thing, but the life of a slave in Kersica was bitter and short. Even those who survived the back-breaking slave masters had much to fear. Each year, on Third Night, thirteen slaves were sacrificed in the name of the gods.

"We will find out soon enough," said Theron. He did not know whether this road led to Kersica, but he would take it.

Theron did not know where the road was going or where it would lead. He only knew it would go on. No doubt this wide dirt path—winding its way through the scrub-filled uplands—had no true end. It would lead through Eloesus and into barbarian lands, through kingdoms and principalities where democracy had not been thought of—all around the circle of the earth until it found its way back to Thénai.

The sky had begun to darken and the sun, to recede. Only a handful of passersby had met them. There was no sign of any village or town. Fear sank in with the setting sun—the knowledge that the furry beasts and the other predator were stalking them. The moon had never looked so radiant. He had lost all fear of lions and bears—the only thing that terrified him, he had already seen.

He gripped his spear. There was fear written in Phaido's eyes. Yet they had to sleep. "We have to alternate watches," he said. "I will go first."

Phaido unraveled his bedroll and struggled inside. He shut his eyes but sleep would not come easy to him—that much, Theron knew.

The crickets were chirping their nightly chorus and out of the mountains, a cold wind blew.

"Theron," he thought he heard the wind say, yet he was not afraid.

He turned to the direction it was blowing—south, to the mountains. No, it came from the east. He breathed in the chill air. It rejuvenated him, exorcised his summer malaise. He walked in its direction.

"Theron," the wind said. "Hero."

Against the wind he walked, until he came to a high precipice. Something like a woman was floating in the air. She was naked but in her hand she covered her breasts with a cloth, white and bright as the moon. A crown of stars was on her head. A serpent was twined around her left arm; its dark eyes peered at Theron as a forked tongue periodically emerged, tasting the air.

"Who are you?" said Theron.

"The wind," said the woman. "That is what you call me. I am waiting for you… in Mount Hylea, in the Sacred Temple. The fate of Eloesus is in your hand, hero…"

This could not be. Mount Hylea was far away, impossibly far. And how could the fate of Eloesus be in Theron's hand? Was there any hand less suitable?

The wind was dissolving the woman—bits of her image began to blow away, dissipating into the night air. She had just been an illusion. When she was gone the wind stopped and its refreshing chill vanished. Theron felt vanquished, and utterly alone.

The sound of stamping feet echoed through the hills, several dozen at a time. Theron's heart froze. He bolted back to his friend, Phaido, who he had left alone.

~

When he came to the place where his friend slept, the sound of stamping feet was mixed with loud grunts and shouts. He kicked Phaido, who woke with a start. He let out a scream and grabbed his walking stick—small comfort in the face of the crazed beasts. They would tear Phaido limb from limb—Theron, too, if he gave them the chance.

OUTSIDE THE WHITE GROTTO

Phaido's heart exploded in his chest. Panic consumed him at the thought of the beasts. He did not want to be eaten. Of all the wretched ways to die, this was the worst of all, the most painful, the most terrifying.

He wondered what the great heroes of myth would have done. Would Phillipidēs stand firm with his spear and shield, longing for nothing more than fame—risking his life for it? Would Alexara dip her sword into stygian waters and drive them away in bursts of light?

What would Phaido do? That much was clear—whimper and cry out in fear, praying to any god or spirit that would listen for safe rescue.

He could see glimpses of their brown fur in the moonlight and the dim yellow outline their eyes. They were like men in some ways—two arms and two legs. But they did not walk upright, nor did they speak—only grunt and roar. They were like the wild men of legend, the men with a giant's strength and a beast's mind.

They were not stepping any closer. Instead they roared and leapt up and down, glaring at Phaido with yellow eyes. Something was holding them back—something they feared. Could they be afraid of Phaido? Perhaps the sight of Theron's spear terrified them.

There was a rustling in the brush behind them. Phaido gasped and whipped around, tripping on his own leg and hitting the hard grassy earth. Theron peered into the darkness, seeing nothing.

How long the night wore on was impossible to tell. The creatures had stampeded away at one point, running for the mountains. At some point Phaido fell asleep—and woke up in the morning light.

The sunlight reflected on the mountains, turning their snowy peaks to dawn shades of gold and pink. Phaido's stomach growled. Theron—he could see—was already up.

Theron handed him a dry morsel, a bit of road bread not fit to be called a meal. "Our last," he said. "Enjoy it."

Phaido took it and ate the dry, tasteless biscuit. He scanned the sky. The terror of the previous night had been washed away by the sun's light.

They had come to a fork in the road—one continued through the hills, another bent southwards toward the mountains. "Where shall we go, Theron?"

"We can't go on like this," said Theron.

Phaido nodded.

"We must find the safety of a village—a village with walls."

Phaido did not trust in walls, not with these beasts following them. No doubt they could climb like spiders and snatch Phaido and Theron from their beds. "Why are they after us?" he said. None of it made sense. It seemed unfair. He had never seen nor heard of such creatures. What had he done in his life to deserve this? Why did the gods curse him? Why did they despise him? He had no talent nor skill. He had been exiled. And now his paltry life would be taken from him, in the worst possible way.

"Why," repeated Theron. "There is no reason to ask why. We must do something about it."

"Which way?" said Phaido.

"You choose," said Theron.

He had once played the part of an old man and had said in the course of the play, "The wise man's hand leans always to the right."

The silly phrase might lead them down a dark path, into the

hands of the crazed beasts. It was no matter.

"It is decided," said Theron. "To the right we go…"

They turned right—southwards—in the direction of the mountains.

~

As they continued down the path in the light of the day, statues began to appear along the road—of a woman with three faces, one young, one old, one ancient. All the statues were in exact proportions, identically carved, and yet painted in different colors. Some faces were olive in complexion like the Eloesians, others white and bloodless like the Isteroi, and some dark red like the Khazidees.

The road was ascending, that much was clear, and the mountains were getting closer. The ground became rocky, more stone than earth. Pines appeared, and well watered streams. The air turned crisp. Late in the day, when the sun was low in the sky, the roar of a rushing stream became evident. At the last leg of the journey, they made one last steep ascent and came to a grotto.

THE WHITE GROTTO

A cave had appeared before them, and out of it flowed a stream. Its dark gray stone contrasted starkly with the white pebbles of the ground below. Above the cave mouth were letters in archaic Eloesian script.

"M-I-R-A, it says." Phaido appeared to be interested but fear strained his voice.

They had been led to a shrine in the mountains, all by itself, with no town or village in sight. They were doomed.

Phaido met Theron's gaze. "I am sorry."

"There is nothing to be sorry about," Theron said. It was true—how would Phaido have known? That did not change the fact that the monsters would surround them, tear them apart with their bare hands, and pick their flesh raw.

Theron gripped his spear. It was well made, with a strong shaft and a long, sharp blade. He had not tried to fight them in earnest. He would get his chance. Perhaps, by some miracle of the gods, he could overcome them. It was unlikely, but maybe it was possible.

"I am sorry," said Phaido. "We are alone. Utterly alone."

Theron wasn't so sure about that. The sun was beginning to dip below the horizon, setting in spectacular colors over the horizon below. The rosy light glittered on the barely-visible sea. Somewhere along the shore was the city they had left behind, Thénai—the only place he had ever known.

He thought of the vision, of the woman and the snake twined around her arm. He wondered if it had any credence, any basis in fact. There was a temple in Mount Hylea, that much was true, but it had lain abandoned for many decades. All rites to that mysterious god which lived on the mountain had ceased. Where once the ancient kings and later, despots, of Eloesus had sought counsel, now no one visited. The god and the priestess who foretold the future were both gone forever, and they would never come back.

A wind was blowing, cold and crisp, hinting of the coming winter rains. Up here, perhaps snow would fall. But there were weeks of summer yet left. The heat would linger. Theron did not want to think of that cold, grim time.

As the wind scattered pine needles, blowing them into the rushing stream, figures appeared—brown furred, mangy and yellow-eyed. Theron gasped and staggered back. Phaido was frozen in fear.

The creatures were armed only with rocks and wooden clubs, yet their strength was beyond doubt. Even if they had been unarmed, Theron had no doubts these dozens and dozens of creatures could overpower them and rip them limb from limb.

"What do you want?" cried Phaido. Desperation strained his voice.

"Mantle!" roared one especially large creature. His brown mane was giant, as large as a lion's, and his eyes had a crazier, more feral look than the others. "Where is mantle?"

"Mantle," Phaido breathed, exasperated. "What are you talking about?"

Theron grabbed his spear in both hands. He had fought and killed before—but with a shield and armor of bronze, locked in step with his fellow hoplites in a phalanx. He had never killed by himself. He had put away the trappings of the hoplite, hoping to never use it again.

There were more than dozens—there were at least a hundred, emerging out of the scattered pines. There was no chance Theron could overcome these creatures, not by himself. He had to flee—but how?

"Mantle!" the creatures' leader shouted. He held a giant

stick, which he beat into the earth. "Where is mantle?"

"We don't have a mantle!" Theron cried.

The leader of the creatures barked some indecipherable curse. His yellow eyes blazed wide. He ground his teeth together—rotted brown stumps the color of his fur. "Then we kill! Kill!"

"Kill!" a dozen repeated.

"Kill!" they shouted in unison, and then began to swarm.

"Run, Phaido!" said Theron.

But he did not. "I am with you to the end," said Phaido.

Something flew overhead—not a bird, but an animal. It hit the ground—not an animal, but a man. No, a woman. She was clad in leather, head to toe, with a pair of black boots that rode high to her knees. In her right hand she held a glaive, and in her left she was spinning a disk—no, the legendary chakrams of the amazon people.

She thrust her glaive forward, piercing a wild creature straight through, then hurled the chakram, taking off the head of another. The creatures were fleeing and screaming, running away down the mountainside before disappearing among the pines.

The amazon kicked the impaled creature off her glaive, and before it hit the earth, beheaded it with the blade. "Run!" she shouted. "Run from this sacred place, foul beasts!"

Two creatures had fallen by her hand in the span of moments. When she turned to face Theron he jerked back and almost fell.

Her face was serious and humorless. Her hair was dark brown, darker than her suntanned skin, and her eyes were bright blue. She had the look of an amazon. She was pretty, in her own way, but not anything Theron was interested in. A man who loved an amazon was liable to be cut in half, or emasculated in the bedroom. "I've been following you two fools," she grunted.

"A pleasure to meet you as well," laughed Theron.

Her face remained grimly serious. "Before you ask, I am Zoë. You owe me your lives."

"Who were those creatures?" said Phaido.

"The trogs?" said Zoë. She walked away and retrieved her bloody chakram. "They are your worst enemy. They are seeking the Mantle of Abraxas. Why they thought you have it, I do not know. Troglodytes are not very smart. I've been following you for days and I could tell you didn't have it."

"Troglodytes," said Phaido, a trace of recognition touching his voice.

THE WHITE GROTTO

Troglodytes were said to be the creations of Kronos, the gods' enemy, lord of chaos and entropy. Phaido recognized the name from the myths, but he had never heard their physical description. Like all the creatures of myth which had appeared in Eloesian drama, Phaido had assumed them to be false. *The moderns are ever-so disparaging of the ancients.*

"What is the Mantle of Abraxas?" said Theron.

It was a wonder that Theron did not fear this amazon. Had he not heard the stories and wives' tales about them? Had his mother not told of the amazons' viciousness, of their hatred of human men and, especially, Eloesian ones?

"Don't ask me stupid questions," said Zoë. "I am merely tolerating your presence. The trogs have an interest in you… that is enough to pique mine. You must know of the Mantle. Where did you see it? Did you touch it?"

"No," answered Theron.

Zoë growled some curse. "Don't waste my time with lies! The trogs have fled but they'll come back in greater numbers…. Numbers that even I can't overcome."

"We aren't wasting your time," said Phaido. "At least, we're not trying to."

Zoë cursed again. She spat onto the ground. "By Amara! You Eloesians are so stupid."

It seemed strange that the amazons worshiped Amara, the same god as the Thenoans did—both as the goddess of wisdom and war, but in dramatically different ways. The amazons, for one, took her aspect as the War Maiden seriously, and they downplayed the annoying bits about her "motherly love" and compassion.

"We must go at once," said Zoë. "This is a sacred place but the trogs have no respect for sacred things."

"Will we go to the mountains?" said Phaido.

Zoë glared. "Their place is in the mountains, fool. Kronos is known as the Mountain Lord."

"Where are we going, then?" said Phaido.

"Kronos intends to destroy the amazon people," said Zoë. "He seems very interested in you two dimwits, for what reason I'll never know. But you are coming with me nonetheless."

"To where?" Phaido said.

"To Mount Hylea, where my goddess lives…"

"Mount Hylea," breathed Phaido. Of old, the tallest peak of Themuria had a sacred temple and a great high priestess… it had been the holiest place of an ancient goddess of light. But its priestess was gone, now, as was her serpent ally. No longer did the blind, mad woman predict the future or counsel princes and kings. No longer were the drums heard on the slopes of the Mount of Prophecy. "The amazons worship Amara," he said. "Why would you take us to that place?"

The hatred and scorn in Zoë's eyes reached a fever pitch. She clearly viewed Phaido as the lowest of all creatures, more despicable than worms and insects. "My people worship Amara… at least, some do. But many remember the old faith."

Phaido feared that glaive of Zoë's, that row of chakrams like rings around her arm. She could overcome them both in a moment's span. They were powerless to stop her; they had to comply… to go to wild, snowy Themuria high in the mountains, and see the ancient temple which hovered above the clouds.

THE HIGH ROAD, OUTSIDE KERSICA

These humans had proven all the assumptions back home—human men were weak and dull-witted and prone to ask stupid questions. They also had little respect for the gods or the matters of heaven and lived in dissolution and drunkenness. How many times had that stupid musician complained about the lack of wine? How many times had his brash fool of a friend sized Zoë up, having lacked the company of human women for so long?

They had left the highlands and taken the High Road, which led from the lowland coast up into the high country of Themuria—what was anciently called Miraea. They were not far from the sea—Zoë thought she could smell the salt in the air. Tall palms grew along the road and the air was stiflingly hot.

Along the flat coastal plain, commerce was evident. Merchants passed them by each mile, along this well traversed road—though few dared take it to its far eastern, high-mountain terminus. The sun was setting and the two were acting skittish, as Zoë had come to expect of human men. "What is the matter?" she grunted.

"We're near Kersica," said Theron, the dumb brawn to Phaido's meager brains. "The Kersepolans will snatch Eloesians outright and enslave them… free Eloesians, not barbarians!"

Zoë would like to see their fears come true… but they had a task to fulfill, even if they were worthless otherwise. Somehow they had a connection to the Mantle of Abraxas. They were too stupid to realize it, not too deceptive. They were far too stupid to be deceivers.

"And we want to stay at an inn tonight," said Phaido. "We're sick of sleeping on the ground."

"Sick," Zoë sneered. "The ground is fine for sleeping. It builds character. The creepers and crawlers won't hurt you. You must toughen up."

The two weaklings glared at her. "We could go back," said Theron. "We have a choice."

Zoë wouldn't waste precious silver on a bed and hot food. These two bumbling fools weren't going to rob her of her scarce money. "You have a choice, exiles?" she said. In her homeland, in the great city of Ipsos, "exile" was unheard of. The amazons were not soft and weak like the Eloesians. When a punishment merited death, they received it. There was no exile, no prisons or fines for major offenses. Those who deserved crucifixion received it; those who deserved hanging were hanged.

The land beyond the road was flat like much of the coastal plain. They had passed by the mountains just days ago. Zoë had heard much talk of these supposedly "fearsome" Kersepolans—Eloesians who couldn't overcome a single amazonian warrior, even in groups. No doubt they were weak like all these Eloesian men, brash and boastful, but frail as infant amazon girls.

Zoë had not seen any sign of trogs. The wild sons of chaos were as cowardly as they were vicious. They were following Zoë and her two weaklings, but only under the cover of night. Their primitive noses could pick up on scents as well as dogs. They did not need any form of intelligence to track them. Somewhere out in these baking hot plains, the trogs were hiding—in a farmer's field, maybe, or in some squalid cave. More would join them soon—a greater number than Zoë could overcome. Soon, the host would be so numerous that their natural cowardice would be overcome… they would descent on Zoë and her two weaklings as they slept, then rip them apart with their bare claws.

Zoë had witnessed the trogs' cruelty before. She could still remember her blood sister and fellow sword maiden. Chloë was the best person she had ever known. She had slain hundreds of trogs with her saber. And yet their numbers had overcome her… hundreds and hundreds had swarmed her. Zoë had fled. She had survived—but Chloë had been ripped apart, her head mounted on a stick which the trog chieftain Gribblik carried for weeks afterward.

Zoë looked down. She was a coward.

OUTSIDE THE WAYWARD INN

Theron could see it—a red tile roof, sheltered from the baking hot sun, warm inviting windows, the clinking of wine glasses and loud echoes of laughter. The sun was setting and the night cool would arrive, erasing all memory of the burning plains. Tall palm trees grew around the inn, sheltering it, a bit, from the sun. "Zoë… please." The amazon looked despondent; some kind of gloom had overtaken her.

Zoë turned to him. Her glaive was in her hand but she did not look so threatening. Who knew what thoughts were running through her mind? "You want to waste twenty *thalon*? You will owe me."

"Owe you, I will," said Theron.

Inside, sheltered from the sun, the Wayward Inn was wonderfully cool. Dozens of travelers sat in the common room, filling every table except one. Wine flowed like rivers from the serving girls' bottles, filling up glass after glass.

The innkeeper settled them in for fifteen silver *thalon* – Theron owed Zoë less than she had thought. A serving girl came by, a striking lass with curly brown hair and an hourglass figure. She wore a skirt that ended above her knees, something that didn't belong in Kersica, with its legendary conservatism and its rejection of luxury. They were in a different world, now, a humorless and harsh world where obedience was demanded and strength was prized above all.

"Wine?" said the serving girl.

"No," said Zoë.

"Yes," Theron corrected her.

Phaido laughed.

"A bottle of red Thelosian, vintage of 299? Only one gold *oros*."

"*No wine*," Zoë boomed.

The powerful voice sent her scurrying away.

"No wine, no laughter when we're with Zoë," said Theron. "Humor and good spirits are distractions from our harsh, boring life."

Zoë glared. Theron wondered if she lacked the capacity to laugh. "Wine is for weaklings," she said. "If they had firewater, I might have it."

Theron had heard of the tasteless, throat-burning drink of the amazons. "Let's have some."

Zoë's glare intensified. "If you had just a drop, Theron, you'd be staggering to your room."

"That sounds fine to me," said Theron. He snapped his fingers. "Hey, hey, lass!"

The serving girl approached again, clearly afraid of Zoë.

"We will have three glasses of firewater," Theron said.

"We don't have any, I'm sorry," said the serving girl. "Are you from the Amazon Isles?"

"No," said Theron.

"Where are you headed?" said the serving girl. "I hope not Themuria… follow this road all the way and it takes you there. I have heard nothing but dark tidings!"

"What kind of dark tidings?" said Theron.

"We are not going to Themuria," snapped Zoë. She was a terrible liar. "We are going to Korthos… to make an offering to Amara…"

Theron wanted to throttle her. Amara was not honored in Korthos—everyone except an amazon would know that.

"Amara?" said the serving girl. "Funny that! Will you be having dinner? We have roast lamb and fresh baked bread... olive oil for dipping, too. And white cheese, too!"

"We have brought road bread," said Zoë.

Theron sighed. Zoë clearly saw no value in good food. He supposed road bread was better than starving.

The serving girl and the innkeeper were chatting amongst themselves quietly, eyeing Zoë.

~

Theron awoke that night with a gasp. He had been overcome by a vicious nightmare of a black mountain with fire pouring from its peak, of a dark demon with horns and burning eyes, of ash and stone raining from the sky and the hissing poison vapors spreading through the air.

The cool air was gusting through the first-story window. He could hear something outside, above the chirping crickets and the hooting owls. Footsteps—and wild, jabbering language. *Trogs.* Theron hurried out of bed to shut the window and found Zoë already there, a chakram in hand, without her armor, in her nightclothes.

"They likely won't attack us in here," said Zoë. "They don't take risks. They fear there are warriors with swords. But you saved our skin, Theron... if we had slept out in the open they would have attacked. They must have swelled their numbers by the thousands."

"What do we do now?" said Theron. Even though they were safe, his stomach had twisted to knots.

"We never camp in the open again," said Zoë. "We seek protection in towns, or inns. But one day that will not be enough. We will only be fully safe when we reach the Mount of Prophecy... and then, only a while."

Theron had never felt so in danger. "They know we don't have the Mantle… why are they still following us?"

"They are convinced that somehow, you know where it is," said Zoë. "They will kill me and take you back to their master…. They will torture it out of you."

Theron gasped and fell to his knees. He feared nothing more than torture. "Will you protect me, Zoë?" He sounded like such a weakling, but who else did these "trogs" fear? They certainly did not fear him.

Zoë's face was illuminated by the sun. In the pale light, something like a smile formed on her face. "I will do my best, Theron."

The light awoke him and yet the sun had not banished his fear. Theron did not want to go outside. Many miles awaited him on this journey, many days and weeks, perhaps months.

~

That day and the next, they stopped at inns. The first time, Zoë allowed them some wine. The next, she had some herself.

"My," she said in the candlelight of the High Rock Tavern, "I see why you like it."

THE HIGH ROAD, OUTSIDE NAUTILOS

The town of Nautilos was now small and insignificant, dominated by the militaristic Kersepolans. Its walls had been cannibalized to create houses—besides, the Kersepolans didn't like their subjects to have any defense.

Phaido couldn't believe the great epic poet Arkelaios had once lived here, or the geographer Laocon. Once Nautilos, in the shadow of the mountains, had been second only to Tharta in Eloesus. Now it was a distant hundredth or thousandth, perhaps even behind the backwater farming villages surrounding Thénai.

"The town has seen better days," said Phaido.

Zoë glanced at him. "We will not stop here," she said. "The day is young. I think there are inns along the road, if my memory serves me well."

Ahead, the road ascended upward. Mountainous hills lay ahead of them, and great snowcapped peaks further beyond. The mountains in the east of Eloesus were the tallest in the world, and what lay beyond them no one knew—the geographer Laocon had died trying to find out.

"You *think* there are inns along the road?" repeated Theron.

"You have traveled many weeks with me," said Zoë. "Trust me."

"How can I trust you if even you aren't sure?" said Theron.

He was terrified of the trogs. Any reasonable person was, but Phaido tried to focus on other things besides his fear. That way he did not envision the wild, yellow-eyed creatures of chaos, the cannibalistic sons of an ancient god—Kronos, demon lord of cruelty and entropy.

"Come on," Zoë said and walked ahead. After moments of

hesitation, Theron followed, spear in hand.

The ground began an uneven but steady ascent, heading up and down hills but taking them higher and higher. By noon, pine trees had begun to replace the familiar holm oaks and dry brush, and many lush pebbly streams were visible, flowing down from the mountains. Peaks higher than any Phaido had seen appeared before him, glistening with snow even in the heat of summer.

"Have you been to Themuria, Zoë?" said Phaido. The unspoiled wilderness was a favored topic of poets and musicians—even, perhaps especially, those who had never been there.

"Once," said Zoë. "It is a beautiful place… wild and lush, but not without its dangers. I went there before the temple was restored… before the oracle and the cosmic serpent returned."

"Where did you hear about her?" said Phaido. He had heard no such thing about the ancient, forgotten temple on the slopes of Mount Hylea.

"I saw her," Zoë said, "in a dream."

"I saw her, too," said Theron.

"What?" cried Phaido.

"We are tied together, then, Theron," said Zoë, "in things we do not know. The priestess of Mira, the Threefold Mother of Light…"

"That is what she is?" said Theron.

Phaido had known the priestess on the Mount of Prophecy worshiped an ancient god, but he had not heard the name Mira before—not until he saw the words etched above the White Grotto. He did not know the words were the name of a goddess, the name of a deity once widespread throughout Eloesus, honored above Amara. "I have not seen her," said Phaido.

Zoë looked back at him. "You will see her soon enough."

After the day had grown late, it was clear they were the only people on the road for miles. An unsettled feeling began to grow in Phaido's stomach. He had not seen an inn for miles and the sun had grown low in the sky. They should have stayed in Nautilos. They should have inquired there about inns along the road. They should have done many things—but what good was hindsight, now?

Theron looked back frequently, eyeing the dark pines, clearly afraid but unwilling to admit it. He had his spear in his hand. No doubt he wished he wore the standard armor of an Eloesian hoplite—a thick bronze breastplate, a round wooden shield, and a helmet with a towering horsehair crest that made him seem tall.

At least he had a spear—Phaido had only a dagger, and barely knew how to use it. Perhaps he could take his lyre and play a song to the troglodytes, a song so irresistible that they forgot their violent nature and realized their common brotherhood with man.

He laughed under his breath.

~

When the sun began to set over the lush pinelands, it was clear no inn was in sight. It was a virtual certainty that the trogs were following them.

"What will we do?" said Phaido.

"We will take the high ground," said Zoë. She was eyeing a high rocky outcrop, a small ridge that extended from the mountains and became a flattop stone hill. "We will alternate watches. We must not show fear. Fear draws them in. They are natural cowards. If they think we fear them, they will feel safe."

Once they had completed the exhausting climb and settled

in along the hill, Zoë took out large pieces of road bread and together they ate, devouring the hard, tasteless morsels and washing them down with water. They had eaten poorly all these many weeks. Phaido had dreamed many times of his old diet, of crispy roast pork and giant glasses of wine. Then he had woken up hungry with a stomach full of dry, unleavened road bread and water.

"I will take the first watch," said Zoë.

Phaido unraveled his bedroll. He knew it would be difficult, if not impossible, to sleep. He sang in the dark of the night to soothe everyone's nerves, especially his own—songs of Phillipidēs, the greatest soldier of the Megarine War, son of the god Alabastros and a human woman. He had fought the Megarans without regard for his life, seeking nothing more than "the fame imperishable," the eternal remembrance of history. He had gotten his wish. "Hail Phillipidēs!" Phaido sang. "Hail Phillipidēs!"

Yet Phillipidēs had fallen. By sorcery, the Queen of Megaris had discovered his weakness—the magic helmet he wore. In the night a spy slipped into the camp and stole the helmet. The next day Phillipidēs was pierced through-and-through with the spear, yet he received what he wanted, "the fame imperishable." His name would never be forgotten.

Phaido did not sing of the death of Phillipidēs. Death was all around him. Neither Phaido nor Theron would receive imperishable fame. It was doubtful Zoë would. Soon his song stopped. There was rustling in the pines below. But eventually his eyes shut, and the weariness of the journey caught up to him. He fell asleep.

~

In the pitch blackness he was awoken by a strong hand—Theron's. "It's your turn," he said. "There has been no sign of them, yet."

Phaido, still exhausted, sat up from his bed. He unsheathed his dagger, though it was small comfort. The short blade would do nothing against the hordes of troglodytes. They were out there, in the predawn hours. Of that there could be no doubt.

Alone with his thoughts, Phaido stood up. The air was horribly cold and Phaido's thick clothing barely kept him warm enough. Up here, near the peaks of the mountains, the winters would be brutal—and winter was coming soon.

Many slow minutes passed, turning to hours in the cold. Phaido expected the glorious sun to arise at any moment, banishing all his fears—and then he heard the first jabber.

"Gribblik!" it sounded like. *"Gribblik!"*

Shadows were moving below, in the pines. He recognized the shaggy manes, the thin, gaunt forms. Icy fear shot through his veins, turning quickly to panic. "Zoë!" he shouted. "Zoë!" Zoë was their only hope. Theron wasn't half as skilled as Zoë.

Zoë sprung out of bed, grabbed her glaive and scooped up all the chakrams that had been laid around her bedroll. She kicked Theron, who woke with a start and—perhaps hearing the jabbering trogs—gasped. He fumbled out of his bedroll, not nearly as nimbly as Zoë, and grabbed his spear. Usually it took him the better part of an hour to wake—a long process of cursing wildly and growling under his breath. Now he was awake instantly, eyes alert with fear. He grabbed his spear.

All Phaido had was a measly dagger. He had bought it on this very journey and had practiced but a little. Its long blade was pointed and sharp, drawing blood easily, as he had found out. It was precious little comfort to hold a blade in his unskilled hands.

The troglodytes were grunting and gabbing. *"Muuuuirrrghul"* they howled. *"Muuirghul Gribblik gribble!"*

"Gribblik," Zoë said as if the word held meaning. The

moon reflected on her face, a face filled with a new anger. She ran to the edge of the stony outcrop without a trace of fear. Phaido followed her, thinking of Phillipidēs. *To face death without fear,* a biographer wrote, *is the most noble of goals, the ultimate sign of character.*

"You want them?" cried Zoë. "You will have to get through me! And I've heard your foul name, Gribblik! You will die and so will all your minions. For Chloë's sake, and mine!"

Who was Chloë, Phaido wondered. There was no time to wonder. Phaido shook his dagger at the gangly creatures below. He spat at them and cursed at them. He was playing his part as an actor—he had become fearless Phillipidēs, who faced death knowing he would be remembered forever. "Come and get me, spawn of the night!" Phaido shouted. "I'll cut you to ribbons! I could do it blindfolded!"

The trogs were hesitating. Could his act be convincing? At last, had his dabblings in drama borne fruit?

ARGON'S TABLE, OUTSIDE THEMURIA

Theron wanted to slam the butt end of his spear into Phaido's jaw. Taunting these foul creatures would only serve to anger them and drive them up the outcrop. Phaido thought he was helping—the idiot!—but he was only quickening their demise. Theron hustled over to the edge opposite Phaido and Zoë and confirmed his worst fears—they were surrounded. "Gods!" he cursed. They were as good as dead.

They had begun to swarm over the rock; Zoë was beating them back with her glaive, slashing and stabbing, spraying black trog blood on the stone. Theron readied his spear, thought of plunging headlong down all those fathoms and sprinting away, but such a fall would break his legs and the troglodyte swarm would overpower him.

A trog heaved itself onto the rock and made a lunge for Theron. Theron thrust hard, impaling it through its tough, tawny hide like a fish pierced, wriggling, on a fisherman's spear. Cold black blood sprayed onto Theron's face. He kicked the trog off and made a dash at the next one, blocking a blow of its club. He charged until he had driven the trog off the sheer rock face. It hit the ground far below with a bone-crunching snap.

Yellow eyes surrounded them, and the dark shapes below formed a veritable sea around them. They were badly outnumbered and horribly outmatched. They stood no chance against all these trogs, not a single chance.

Behind him, Zoë was unleashing a volley of chakrams, one after the other, lopping off the heads of trogs left and right. Soon she ran out of them. She began backing away, toward the center of the rocky ground, utterly surrounded, utterly alone in the cold mountain night. All Zoë's wild cutting and stabbing could not save them. Theron stabbed furiously with his spear, never managing to stick one like he had before. The trogs were as nimble as they were jumpy, dodging out of the way with each spear thrust. Panic had been replaced with pure adrenaline. The thrill of the fight had returned to him. He had never thought so keenly or quickly. He was in the battle lines again, joined shield-by-shield in the phalanx with his brothers-in-arms—but instead of a brother, a weakling friend and a sister far mightier than he.

"Enough!" howled Zoë. "My glaive has drunk enough blood—you will not show your face, coward Gribblik! So be it!"

She pulled something out of the pockets of her leathers—a sun-shaped disk.

"*Eos!*" Zoë cried. "By Mira, and the Sisterhood of the Sun! *Eos! Eeeeooossss!*"

The sun-shaped disc blazed with light, turning a hundred times the brightness of the sun, turning gold, then yellow, then blue and finally blinding white. It hummed with power, first loud and then deafening. Zoë looked like she was in pain. "*Sola! Mira! Eos!*" She cast the blazing sun disk to the fire and it erupted in a burst of flame which became a hundred-foot tall white inferno. She thrust her glaive into the dazzling fire and it in turn blazed white.

With a new confidence she leapt forward, surefooted as a lion. The trogs fell over themselves to flee, trampling each other underfoot. Some tripped off the outcrop. Others leapt off intentionally. Every one of them ran away, screaming into the night.

Theron could not believe his eyes. "Our Zoë is a sorceress?"

"I am not *your* Zoë," she breathed. "And I am not a sorceress. That was a *solaricon,* fool… an item more costly than the amazon queendom itself. Lives were lost in its making. That was the last one in existence… and I have wasted it."

"Wasted it!" laughed Theron. "You saved our lives."

"A *solaricon* is worth more than our lives put together… no one knows how to make them anymore. It is said a dozen priestesses of Mira lost their lives in each one's making."

Theron knew many amazons worshiped the sun.

"Others say they are an artifact of the Old Dominion," continued Zoë.

"And what do you say?" Theron asked. The fire was still blazing, hot yet not burning them. The flicker of white flame had left Zoë's glaive.

"I say a precious treasure has been lost by my hand," said Zoë. "The last of the *solaricons*… all for three small lives. It was a gift to me by the High Priestess, the chief of the Solarines. I have put it to poor use."

"There's no time to dwell on it," said Theron.

"Perhaps we should continue down the road," suggested Phaido.

"Fools, the both of you," snapped Zoë. "You do not understand the loss. And going up the road is your most bone-headed suggestion yet, Phaido. The trogs won't return here for weeks, not even after the *solaricon's* fire dies down. Enough! Away with you! I must mourn, if you won't. I will be back in the morning." Again she plunged her glaive into the column of white fire. The blade blazed brighter than before, seeming to burn and glow. "Avast! *Eos! Mira! Sola!* A dark day for the world and for amazon-kind." The column of fire burst with new energy, blazing high into the sky. Zoë leapt down the rock face and disappeared.

Theron did not understand the loss, but now he knew it was great.

~

The sunlight bathed Theron in warmth and the chirping of the birds awoke them. The column of fire still burned, showing no signs of quieting, and in brightness it equaled the sun. Zoë had returned, a sense of gloom and loss having overtaken her features. Her frown, it seemed, was permanent. Phaido sat away from her, by himself, not daring to speak. It seemed Theron, as always, was the last one up.

"I am sorry for your loss," said Theron. He struggled out of his bedroll.

"Enough words, Theron," said Zoë. "Your empty platitudes mean nothing to me. It is the world that has lost, and not amazon-kind. Speak one more angering word and I will thrust you into the fire… It will devour you in seconds."

"Maybe I'll push you in," said Theron.

Zoë glared like she had never glared before. "I could toss you in without any effort. I'll show you how we amazons deal with boastful human men."

"Stop!" cried Phaido. "We are in danger enough. We don't need to add hatred between ourselves to the troubles."

Zoë's angry glare remained. Her voice was calm when she spoke: "Very well, Theron. Phaido. The singing fool speaks the truth. There is an army of trogs out there, and we must hike fast to safety. There are dangers in the mountains, too, besides."

~

The pace increased twofold and Zoë led the pack. The twisting mountain roads wound higher and higher, leading them besides babbling brooks filled with cold water and great clusters of pine trees. The air grew thin. As the day wore on a sudden thunderstorm rained down upon them, but was gone seconds later. Several times, Theron spied a deer—does all, but much larger than those on the coast. They were reaching a far country, a wild and unspoiled wilderness. Phaido had sung before in his strained voice of the wild Arkadian woods, the gushing waters, the tall pines and the winter snows.

The sun had begun to dip and the upward-leading road had begun to taper off. Here, at the roof of the world, the air was thin yet unspoiled by the smoke and odors of human habitation. Theron had never seen such greenery—the pines, the well-watered grass, the bushes and hedges.

"Where are we?" said Phaido.

"Many days from Arkadion," Zoë said.

"*Days?*" cried Phaido.

"Days," said Zoë. "Maybe weeks. The Themurian wilds are empty, save of deer and wolves and bears…"

Theron grumbled some curse. Why had he agreed to accompany Zoë? In a way, she had saved them. In other ways, she had been their downfall. She had taken them here, for one—to a wilderness far from the safety of human company. No walled towns or great cities of the low-lying coast, just dense forests and bubbling springs.

"I hear pipes," Phaido said. A wide smile formed on his face. "People…"

When Theron focused, he could hear it, too. There was more than one piper and the melody was so striking he could not help but begin to dance.

"Stop it," said Zoë. "You are not hearing people. They are forest spirits… revelers… You know them as satyrs. Their melody makes a person forget himself…"

At the pointed remark, Theron stopped his dancing.

"They are rambunctious when they manage to steal wine," said Zoë. "And when they want to, they can pipe a person into danger, lead her into the wild, teasing her with the melody but drawing her further and further away…"

The satyrs of Themuria were a legend across the land. Some claimed they were hallucinations of small minds, affected by the cold climate, but others claimed to have seen them—furry manes, pointed ears, and cloven hooves all.

Theron readied his spear just in case.

"They won't come close to us," said Zoë. "Your spear is worthless. Just don't make too much noise—otherwise they might realize they have a human to trick."

~

The sun was beginning to set and Zoë handed out the road bread—an already-bland meal they had gotten sick of. Theron forced it down and sipped some water from his canteen. Doom was settling over them, over the pines, the rocks, the boulders and the stones.

"The trogs—" whimpered Phaido.

"The trogs will fear us for days," said Zoë. "You have nothing to worry about tonight except your own cowardice. They will not risk attacking us… they think we might have more *solaricons*."

Theron silently thanked Phaido for bringing up the dreaded topic—and accepting Zoë's stern reprimand like a sacrificial lamb.

"We must sleep," said Zoë. "Actually, *you* must sleep. I will take the first watch."

THEMURIA, MILES FROM NOWHERE

Zoë had spoken overconfidently to soothe their weak human minds. It was highly unlikely that the trogs would attack after the incident with the *solaricon,* but not impossible. The greater their numbers, the bolder their actions. No doubt, more trogs from the outlying mountains were joining them now. An excess of a thousand filthy trogs pursued them, probably—all seeking these two dimwits, who didn't even understand their connection to the Mantle of Abraxas. Precious little thinking went on within those skulls of theirs. If a trog smashed their head, would any gray matter fly out at all, or just a tiny strand?

The seconds turned to minutes, the minutes to hours. In the cool air and her warm leathers, Zoë had never been quite so comfortable. She shut her eyes once, then twice. Her blinks grew longer. Soon she had fallen asleep.

THEMURIA, MILES FROM NOWHERE

Theron jolted awake at the sound of sizzling thunder and a flash of blue. *A storm,* he thought, but there was no rain. There was screaming—the panicked sounds of trogs. He grabbed his spear, not bothering to wake snoring Zoë, and followed the light. She would just make a mess of things, anyway.

The pines fell away behind him, revealing a rocky high meadow.

Dark shapes—trogs—were fleeing in terror from the form of a giant. He had to be thirty feet tall. His body was covered in a gold breastplate, save his giant arms, and in his hands he gripped a hammer glowing white. His eyes were blue and flaming, and around him the air seemed to hum and crackle with energy. On his head was a winged helm, and lightning struck at random around him, sizzling in the air.

A hand grabbed Theron and yanked him to the floor. "Fool!" Zoë snapped. "Don't anger the titan when he's doing our work for us!"

Theron had had enough of her. Zoë's constant commands, mixed with her petulant anger, awoke something inside of him. He pushed her away, slamming her into the ground—Zoë, an amazon, three times his strength.

"A titan!" he cried, loud enough for the trogs to hear, and watched the battle like a show at the theater.

The titan was shouting as it swung its bright white hammer. The words were indistinguishable—the tongue of lightning and thunder, the speech of black clouds and pouring rain.

Zoë tackled him. She wrestled with her, thinking of the legendary Phillipidēs who wrestled with a god and won. If he, only a demigod, could overcome Alabastros, surely Theron could overcome Zoë.

It was clear Zoë had twice his strength. He squirmed and wormed away, wriggling out of Zoë's death grip as her hands became sweaty. He stood up and grabbed his spear, which he realized he had dropped. He thrust his spear forward, within an inch of her throat. She reached for her glaive but Theron pushed his spear further forward, until the blade was pushing against her skin.

A change came over Zoë then, as she met his gaze. Theron saw something in those dark eyes he thought he'd never see… respect. "Well done," said Zoë. "Now let me go."

"Why should I?" said Theron playfully.

"Look behind you."

The titan was running at them. The earth shook at each step. The lightning flame in his eyes was burning and he was pitching back his hammer.

Zoë snapped to her feet, grabbed her glaive, and hurled it. The weapon whistled through the air and then spiked into the titan's head. Instead of blood, liquid fire emerged from the wound, burning bright. The titan roared, and yanked out the glaive. The lightning around him stopped its sizzling. His face had become a mask of liquid fire. He ran away as fast as he had charged, leaving them behind.

Zoë ran to grab the glaive. At the sight of Zoë, the titan slayer, even the brave trogs who had waited in the shadows panicked, fleeing into the night.

~

"Never flee from a titan," said Zoë as they walked back to camp. "You can never outrun one."

"Lesson learned," said Theron.

"I will take the last of the night's watch," Zoë said. "I won't be able to sleep again."

THEMURIA, MILES FROM NOWHERE

Days had passed, or was it weeks, or years?

Still they were the only travelers along the winding road. The poets of old had written much of the "Arkadian ideal," Phaido knew. They had praised the gushing streams and the lush meadows of the roof of the world. Musicians sang of the piping forest spirits. Composers had tried to record the satyrs' songs, but no human piper could match their skill.

As for Phaido, he had grown to detest the wilderness, the rugged, often stormy days and the cold, often freezing nights. Natural beauty—like the grand snowcapped peaks which surrounded them at every turn—did not inspire Phaido's muse. He took more inspiration from the politics of the lowland coast, from the drinking parties and symposiums of Thénai, and from the music of singers much better than he.

The travel had begun to wear him down. Aches grew in his body which would never be healed, twists and knots in his back that plagued him in his sleep. Sweat and dirt and a lack of bathing had made them all stink terribly. The waters were too cold for bathing.

Zoë said any day, Arkadion would appear—the lone town of Themuria, an isolated outpost that no self-respecting coastlander would ever visit.

Phaido still feared the trogs. They seemed to fear Zoë still, many days after the incident with the *solaricon*. But it was a matter of time before they regained their bravery and attacked them while they camped. They had no chance against so many. One way or another, they walked to their deaths.

OUTSIDE ARKADION

Zoë had begun to worry. Could Arkadion have vanished from the face of the earth? Had the wilderness swallowed it whole? There was only one High Road and it led to Arkadion. There were no forks in the road she could have taken, no mistake she could have made. It had been two weeks, she counted, since the battle with the titan, and still there was no sign of Arkadion, the legendary Bride of the Wilderness.

Then the ground began to descend. The pines descended with it, revealing a lush green valley. Miles away, jutting above the clouds, was a bent peak she recognized on amazonian coins—Hylea, the sacred Mount of Prophecy.

They descended the downward-sloping road quickly. The pines peeled away to reveal farmland in this high valley—green pastures where cows and sheep grazed, and in some places, plots of wheat newly cut. In the midst of the desolate wilderness was this well-watered, grassy valley. Arkadion had to be close-by.

~

After a long walk, it appeared. The Bride of the Wilderness was a small village, lacking even the most basic walls. Nominally, it had pledged its allegiance to Kersepoli. But who would want it? Zoë couldn't help her disappointment, seeing its timber houses, its humble market square, its wooden temple—she noted—dedicated not to Mira but to Tyros.

ARKADION

Phaido could scarcely contain his excitement. *Arkadion, at last!* There were people here, albeit a strange folk wearing thick woolen clothing and speaking in a peculiar dialect. There was a temple, albeit low to the ground and built of wood. There was a market square—a dirt one, true, but one that sold real goods. There was an inn with food. Their troubles were gone, at least for a night. The Mount of Prophecy could wait, at least until the next day. He would spend a hundred *doukon* just for a hot bath. He would spend a thousand for a glass of wine. *Too bad Zoë holds our purse-strings.*

Villagers idled by the market square. They were glaring at Phaido and Theron, but especially Zoë. It appeared Arkadians did not possess any hospitality.

A man left the doors of the inn, glaring with twice the villagers' intensity. "You flatlanders aren't here to cause trouble, are you?" he sneered in that peculiar Arkadian dialect. "I see you have even brought an *amazon.*"

The mountain rustics did not bother to mask their hatred. A coastlander was bad enough, Phaido thought, but a warrior woman in leathers, not even—by definition—belonging to the human race surely riled these small-minded people. Perhaps they had met coastlanders before who had treated them with well-deserved disdain. Coastlanders, they perhaps thought, were a people with their head in the clouds, with cares beyond the maintenance of cows and sheep and the timing of the first frost.

"We aren't here to cause trouble," Zoë said with surprising politeness. "We mean you no harm. We seek lodging at your inn. We can pay good prices."

"No price is enough to house an amazon," snapped the man who had come from the inn. "You two are humans, right? I hear amazon men are pathetic and weak. You can stay… but not this woman."

"Then none of us will stay," Theron boomed.

"Suit yourself," answered the innkeeper.

"A poor businessman, that," said Phaido.

The innkeeper snarled as he walked back inside. The crowd gathered in the square scattered. Zoë turned to face them. To Phaido's surprise, there were tears forming in her eyes, and her tan face had flushed a shade of red.

"What is wrong?" asked Phaido.

"Swords and spears I can bear," said Zoë. "Titans and trogs I can defeat. But insults… those, I cannot answer."

Was there a touch of tenderness to Zoë's seemingly impenetrable hide? Did these small-minded rustics' hatred for amazons pierce her cold heart?

Theron drew near her. She slapped him away and snarled, "Get away from me!" and the tears shook loose. Clearly she was struggling to restrain her weeping. "We sleep tonight, outside town… then we go to the Mount of Prophecy."

~

They laid their bedrolls outside a pasture as the sun began to set. The lights of Arkadion were behind them, and the cold night was alive with the sound of chirping crickets and night birds. Cold winds gusted down from Mount Hylea every so often, waking Phaido up. They were truly at the roof of the world, far from any form of civilization, far from the cares and worries of Thénai. He no longer worried about the trogs; even they seemed like a distant dream.

NORTH OF ARKADION

The stars had never seemed so bright, nor the moon so white and brilliant. A wind blew from the Mount of Prophecy and the wind spoke: *"Get up!"*

Theron leapt out of his bedroll and onto his feet. Dark shapes were massing all around them. The lights of Arkadion occasionally pierced that distance, bathing with orange light a collection of hairy manes and filthy beards. *Trogs.* He grabbed his spear where it lay by his bedroll.

Zoë was sleeping. Once he had found her intimidating or frightening—but now, with the long time spent with her, and the soft side of her revealed—there was no more beautiful woman in the world. No one else could take her place. Yet their love-making would surely end in Theron's broken bones. An amazon was a black widow spider when it came to love.

Zoë gasped as she fumbled out of her bedroll. As always she wore her leathers, even in her sleeping. She kicked Phaido, grabbed her glaive, and scooped up her dozen chakrams.

"Trogs! Trogs!" she breathed.

The cold wind blew, gusting down from the mountains, freezing in temperature and breath-stealing intensity. The wind spoke again: *"Horses!"*

Theron had seen a stable. "Follow me!" he called out. Zoë and Phaido obeyed after a moment's hesitation. The trogs had begun to charge.

~

In Arkadion the villagers were screaming with fear, some running away, some hiding under barrels or crates. "Look at what the flatlanders have brought to us!" screamed one. It was true. The three of them were the cause of these people's misery. Trogs appeared down every road. Their yellow eyes glinted in the light of candles and torches. "There he is!" growled one, pointing his giant yellow-nailed thumb at Theron.

"Gribblik!" Zoë cried. "Avast! Run, before I cut off your head."

"Ah, the amazon!" cried the trog chief Gribblik. His face was long and mottled with scars, and his filthy brown beard fell to his knees. One eye was bigger than the other, and his skin had the tawny consistency of leather. A horned helmet sat lopsided on his head, refusing to fit—no doubt pillaged from some raid.

He was blocking the door to the stable.

Trogs surrounded them. They refused to attack, not wanting to risk their lives, not wanting to strike until their safety was assured.

"She has no sun-fires left!" grumbled Gribblik. "Attack! Attack!"

But the trogs were unsure.

"Perhaps if you attacked first, and showed them your brave example…" Zoë's words elicited wary laughter from the trogs, but Gribblik was not amused. He regarded Zoë with a burning glare.

"For Chloë!" Zoë cried and unleashed a volley of chakrams—three, in quick succession. One bounced off the stick that Gribblik carried; one sliced a gaping wound in his arm; the other chopped the stick in half.

Gribblik howled and drew twin daggers. He charged and his fellow trogs followed. In the confusion, batting and stabbing with his spear, Theron made his move.

~

He let the horses out of the stables one by one. None had

saddles. These beasts—which could cost a whole *talent* in gold and silver—were free for the taking. One Theron struggled to mount, but only succeeded in scaring away. Hapless he followed the giant beasts as they fled, neighing, into the night.

The trogs ran back at the sight of the horses. Gribblik was bowled over. Zoë cried out, "Thank Mira!" and came running, hopping feet into the air and smoothly mounting the horse. "Up!" she cried. "Up!" and held out her hand. Phaido mounted first. "You will have to do it yourself!" she cried to Theron. "You can do it, Theron… I believe in you!"

A trog was running low, trying to tackle Theron. Theron leapt in the air. His legs hit the horse and he struggled, grasping air, and for a long second thought he might fall. Then he steadied and galloped away, following Zoë down the road, in the direction of Hylea, the sacred Mount of Prophecy.

~

The ride to Mount Hylea was as difficult and terrifying as Theron could have imagined. At least the light of the stars and moon, blazing brighter than he had ever seen them, banished the darkness. And yet that provided its own terrors—namely, the trog chieftain Gribblik pursuing him. The moon's wan light had turned him into a silhouette—a long, lanky body, a horned helmet, riding on a horse, beating the beast furiously and spurring it to go ever faster, faster, faster.

Theron's leg grip was unsteady. He had ridden without a saddle before, but not often. The amazons rode no other way; Phaido was in good hands.

Faster, faster, they rode, into the cold night, to the bent peak of Mount Hylea, to the sacred home of prophecy in the light of the stars.

MOUNT HYLEA

Snow was visible as they ascended the pine-covered peaks—snow, which Theron had never seen up close. The peaks surrounding Thénai were white, and some people he knew—intrepid explorers—had ventured all the way to that freezing, inhospitable place. The moonlight reflected on the patches of white amid the tall green pines, hangers-on from a cold winter.

"Run! Yes, that's right, run!" hollered Gribblik, shaking Theron's reflection and replacing it once more with pulsing fear. "I will bash your brains in one way or the other… just like I bashed your friend's… but not before all my men had a turn with her!"

The response from Zoë was one of stoic silence. It was clear she knew how to handle horses. In the riding and rearing of horses, amazons had no equal. She navigated the treacherous, winding mountain path with ease, guiding her horse and keeping it calm. Theron did his best, but Gribblik clearly had no worries for the beast he rode—with viciousness he beat it, spurring it ever faster and faster. It neighed and whinnied.

Theron looked back; the poor beast's eyes were wild with terror.

The air was growing colder and thinner. Theron's clothes had become insufficient. They were near their destination—and yet Theron could not shake the feeling that they were nearer to their end.

~

Did hours pass? Theron could not tell. Exhausted and shivering with cold, the path ascended its final leg and opened up to reveal a giant clearing where no pines grew, and the ruins of a temple lay. Its pillars were smashed, its roof collapsed. Weeds grew on the dark accursed earth. *There is no priestess,* Theron realized. "We have come for nothing," he said. "We are alone!"

Zoë let out a wail. She stopped her horse on the accursed earth and wheeled it around to face Gribblik. Gribblik halted his in turn. Theron stopped half between them. Zoë's burning glare was evident even in the dim moonlight. Her hatred for Gribblik threatened to bubble over and devour them all.

"Flee from here, son of darkness!" howled Zoë. "This is a holy place… a place of light."

"I ate your friend's brains," said Gribblik. "I sucked the marrow from her bones. We made a pudding from her blood… we ate every bit of her. From her skull I made a cup, from her bones a soup…"

Zoë thrust her glaive into the high mountain air. "Back! Back!" Tears were in her eyes, mourning for her lost friend.

THE RUINED TEMPLE

Zoë wept for her lost hope. The priestess was not here. The temple was empty, as empty as it had been for the past three hundred years. The dreams she had—the visions of the holy Temple of Light—had been nothing more than the delusions of a lost soul. Her hopes trickled away with her tears. Darkness would consume them all. The world was at an end. She had no hopes to fight it.

"My men will be here soon," grumbled Gribblik. "They will take turns with you, Zoë. Then I will eat you flesh from bone. A war chief has privileges."

"Privileges." Zoë spat. She would make a last stand. These two human men—fools and weaklings though they were—had become friends. She realized, though she had no respect for humankind, that she cared for Phaido and Theron. She cared about them as much as Chloë. She did not want them taken to the Crimson Peak; she did not want them tied to a rack and inflicted with unspeakable pain. "Death!" Zoë shouted. "Death to you, Gribblik, and hellfire forever after!"

She flung Phaido from the horse. She gripped her glaive firmly. She sat aright on her horse. Then, remembering Chloë and all the destruction the sons of Kronos had caused, she charged.

Gribblik drew twin knives, which glowed in the light of the moon. He parried her strike and launched himself off his horse. He tackled Zoë, who fell all those feet to the ground. Her body heaved under the pressure. She couldn't breathe. Gribblik cut wildly, slashing her face and her breast. She reached for her glaive but it was not there.

A spear emerged through Gribblik. Theron loomed above her. Gribblik's eyes widened in panic but he was impaled. Phaido, what she had considered the worthless musician, slashed Gribblik's throat with his dagger. Blood was pouring over Zoë, Gribblik's and her own. The horses were nickering nervously. There were others coming. One way or the other, she was dead.

THE RUINED TEMPLE

Theron was weeping as he—together with Phaido—lifted up Zoë's savaged body. She was bleeding profusely and it became clear with each passing moment that there was no hope for her whatsoever. There was no hope for any of them at all. The priestess was nowhere to be found—the only thing to be found was death.

Together they took her into the dark night, with thoughts of trogs on their mind. They took her across the cold mountain clearing into the collapsed temple, the temple of lost hope.

Gribblik was dead by Theron's hand but his fellow trogs were coming. Theron was queasy at the thought of death. He was no Phillipidēs; he was no hero. They reached the marble floor of the temple. Zoë was groaning in the dark of the night. They laid her down, not knowing what to do. Left behind in the temple was a staff, forgotten perhaps by the last pilgrims.

There was loud jabbering. Dark shapes had appeared in the distance, dark shapes easily recognizable as trogs. Theron readied his spear. He was shaking. His gut had twisted to knots. He did not want to die. More than anything, he wanted to live. Zoë wailed.

He looked back; she was slapping the marble floor with her hand. As she bled she groaned. The wooden staff near her was carved in the form of a snake. It seemed she wanted it—a last comfort, perhaps, in death.

The trogs were running at them. Nonetheless he grabbed Zoë's trembling hand and wrapped it around the wooden staff.

There was a bright flash of light. The staff bent and grew scales; it twisted and became lithe and living. The snake twined around Zoë's hand. Theron cried out. He stabbed at the serpent; there was a flash of white light and his spear went flying.

Zoë stood up; no, she was being raised into the air. Her leathers and underclothes fell off her and a white cloth replaced them. Her eyes turned white and sightless; Theron realized all along, Zoë was the woman in his dreams, the woman who had appeared to him in the White Grotto, the woman who spoke through the wind.

"Zoë!" he cried, but she did not respond. Her name was not Zoë anymore. She had become an ascended immortal, a divine being on par with Phillipidēs.

The trogs were fleeing, now, running over the mountainside. They tripped over themselves as they sought to run away. Theron looked back at Phaido, breathless with fear, and saw his friend cowering on the ground, shielding his eyes from the terrible apparition in front of him.

"Hero!" said Zoë. The snake twined around her body let loose its forked tongue.

"Who are you talking to, Zoë?"

"I am Io; I have always been Io," she said. "You are Hero; you have always been Hero."

But Theron was not a hero. If any in their group had been a hero, it was Zoë. "I am not a hero," he said.

"Lies," said Io. "Tell me, Hero, do you love this land? Do you love Eloesus, the place of your birth?"

"I… yes, I suppose."

"You do not love it," Io said. "You must learn to love it. The Hero must love this land if it is to survive."

"How can I love a land that rejected me?" said Theron. At the spoken words he was close to tears.

"You must," said Io, "because the free peoples of Eloesus have no hope without you. Two dooms have been declared upon Eloesus. The first doom is Kronos and his sons; the second is more terrible, and is by human hands. The first requires a spear; the second, unity."

"I don't understand…" Theron fell to his knees.

"In ancient days," said Io, "a demon walked the earth. His name was Kronos, and Abraxas was his deputy. In ancient days, Kronos was slain by the hero Helēmon. In ancient days, Abraxas boiled the demon's blood into a gem, and set it in a cloak… the dark Mantle which contains the demon's power."

Now Theron understood everything. The cloak which he had taken as a spoil of war, the cloak which the archon Epaphras had stolen from him—that was the Mantle of Abraxas, the thing the trogs had been hunting all along. "What happened, then?" said Theron. "Why didn't it destroy me? The demon's-blood gem touched me… why did I not die?"

"The Mantle of Abraxas did not destroy your soul because you are of a greater mettle… you are a hero," said Io. "The blood of Phillipidēs runs through your veins, and many heroes before him."

He could not discount the fact; his father, long dead, had come from a line of rustics far outside Thénai's city walls. He had been incredibly strong.

"Thénai is in danger," said Io. "That danger may well spread far beyond its borders."

"I must go there…"

"Its walls are sealed," said Io, "and the leader of the city has been poisoned against you. You must go to Amazonia and seek the queen herself. No one else can help you."

"The amazons—I can't go without you, Zoë," said Theron.

"Zoë!" cursed Io, "have you gone mad?"

"That was your name once," said Theron.

"In the isle of Jogheira, in the city of Tigris by the shore," said Io, "there you must go. There lies the Eloesians' last hope. Give this to Queen Daphnë. She will know what it means."

Seemingly out of nothing, Io drew a gold medallion without a lanyard. Like a giant coin, it had the bent peak of the Mount of Prophecy forged upon it; on the other side were writings Theron did not recognize—Archaic Eloesian, maybe. "Are you certain?" asked Theron.

Io was dancing in the air as the serpent coiled tight around her arm. Drums were pounding, drums Theron could not see. The high mountain meadow pulsed with music and a supernatural energy.

"Nothing is certain!" cried Io. "Tell the queen of the rise of Kronos… of the Abraxas' Mantle… of the temple re-dedicated, and the goddess's return." Io snarled and bared her teeth. She barked like a wolf. "Go! Arise, my nation! Arise and eat much flesh!"

A wind burst down the mountaintop, cold and bracing. Theron followed the obvious command—to flee, to run away, to return to the lowland kingdom from which he came. The amazons awaited, a people harsher and more dark-hearted than the worst of the Kersepolans. They would tear him limb from limb—but it was clear, after all that had transpired, that Io—the new Zoë—did not care.

THE WARRIOR

Phillipidēs beheld the town
Tall white walls and a gate of bronze—
Megaris where his fortune was!
He beat his sword against his shield
Then cried the brave Phillipidēs,
"Here is fame imperishable!
Here my eternal glory lies!"

—Arkelaios

ARGON'S TABLE

The exhaustion of the journey back had sapped Phaido's willpower. At least, with the coin they had pilfered from the former Zoë's coinpurse, saddles for the horses had been purchased—at the stables in Arkadion, no less. The hostler couldn't pass over the money, despite the heavy protests of the locals.

No wonder, they had reached Argon's Table—where Zoë had unleashed the power of the *solaricon*—before the first snow of winter. They traveled quickly on these beasts, and with much less struggle. They had become rich men, possessing an item worth a *talent* apiece. What would the people of Thénai, who spurned them, think now?

"You know," said Phaido as they passed by the stone table, "we don't have to do what Zoë says. We can go seek safe haven somewhere. The Ten Cities allow in exiles and escaped criminals…" And yet something had changed about his friend. Phaido couldn't put his finger on it. He had become more serious about things. He had lost much of his humor. He was not the vagrant and ne'er-do-well that Phaido had known and loved.

The comment clearly annoyed him. "No," he said, "we have a duty to perform."

Perhaps it was Zoë's lie that had turned him into this new and distasteful creature—that somehow Theron, simple-minded Theron, was related to the great hero Phillipidēs. The idea was preposterous enough that it should have encountered a little resistance in Theron's mind.

There was a rustling in the pines. Phaido had thought the trogs had left them.

~

The treacherous mountain ground flattened out into the burning plains of the coast. Grass surrounded them, gold in color. This giant space had always lacked for water. One had to dig deep wells to survive out here, and no plants would grow. This was the domain of shepherds and goatherds—at least, those who dared to face the heat.

The road forked and Theron led them on westward, away from Thénai their home, and away from the land of Kersepoli, where sale into slavery would be inevitable.

KORTHICA

Days after they had left the mountain lands, a shining sea appeared, sparkling in the sun. At its shore lay a city of incredible size, twice or maybe three times the size of Thénai. Its walls, staggering in their height, gleamed light tan in the sun, and a sea-wall of equal height stretched out north before reaching the port. Here was Korthos, a city like no other, which had lain free of tyrant and autocrat for as long as Thénai. So prosperous were its people and so strong was its military that Kersepoli had failed to vanquish it and bring it under the heel of their ever-expanding empire.

"I can't believe it," said Phaido.

Theron, as ever, was gruff. He said nothing, as Phaido expected, but Phaido wouldn't let him steal his excitement. The greatest city in Eloesus besides Tharta lay before them, a hive of commerce, a center of wealth and entertainment. It was the dream of every actor to grace its stages; it was the dream of every singer to grace its music halls.

Its colonies and overseas dominions were without compare; only Thénai could match their number. Phaido had always been proud of his city, Thénai, at the expense of all others, but how could they ever compete with those walls. They had to be eighty feet tall.

The road became packed with merchants and travelers as they drew near, reaching a peak after having grown more and more crowded in the passing days. Ox carts and horsecarts heavy laden with merchandise rolled ahead, packing amphorae filled with olive oil, Thenoan pottery, silks and spices from Tharta and Ten Cities; and priceless treasurers from around the world.

At the gate a backlogged line had formed, with each

merchant and sightseer forced to make their case to enter Korthos, the famed city of a thousand temples. The process took hours and ended only when the sun had dipped low in the sky. Phaido had grown sweaty and saddle-sore, waiting in the hot sun, when the gatekeeper snapped abruptly, "From where do you hail?"

"Thénai!" said Phaido.

The gatekeeper sneered. "Thénai… I hope you haven't brought your fleas and filth with you."

"It's actually quite clean," said Phaido. The words stung him. He had loved Thénai since the days of his childhood; civic pride had been instilled in him to the core.

"You call it clean?" said the gatekeeper. "You will want to buy some eye balm we've just gotten from the Blessed Isles, good for blindness. The Hymnians have made a splendid concoction… you will be able to see again, and behold the putrid dump heap you live in."

The hurt was replaced with fury. How could he be a proud Thenoan and listen to this filly Korthian speak like this? "We have the highest of the high cities… our temple to Amara stretches to the clouds."

"And our council is making plans to heighten our High City," said the gatekeeper. "Soon it will dwarf your pitiful village and we will be unequaled except by Tharta… Korthos—the greatest library, the largest theater, the highest High City."

Phaido wanted to wrap his hands around the gatekeeper's neck and never stop squeezing. "Greatest library—that is debatable." Korthos had a grand library, a beautiful work of architecture, but Thénai's library was thrice its size, hosting more than a hundred thousand scrolls and books.

"I feel sorry for you, Thenoan," said the gatekeeper, "and in the end that is why I must let you pass… don't stay too long and spread your diseases. *Next!*"

Phaido was fuming as he rode down Korthos' majestic white streets. He had hoped to enjoy the city, to see the famed Temple of Nix, but he could not bear it. The derision was clear. Those who walked the streets and saw an Eloesian on a horse might think he was a Korthian of some import, but if they found out he was Thenoan they would view him as vermin.

The street opened up into a great white square. In the center, beside the well, a crowd had gathered before the sight of a giant statue. It was built of burnished bronze, shaped like an armored man. It reminded Phaido of the titan he had seen in Themuria, except twice as imposing.

"Come one, come all!" shouted a street crier. "The great inventor Agenor has brought his famed colossus! With no effort we will surely bash down the walls of Kersepoli and claim all its territories as our own!"

A wall stood in front of the colossus, thick and built of stone, held fast to the town square through supports.

"A jolt of lightning is all it takes!" the street crier shouted. "Our victory over Kersepoli is sealed!"

He had heard little talk of Tharta, the other great city-state. It was no secret that the Korthians admired Eloesus' first city—the lone state in Eloesus still ruled by a king, as wealthy and well-regarded as it was proud and pompous. The Korthians would use this "colossus" against Kersepoli and surely Thénai, but never Tharta. They were forever Tharta's lapdog.

"Watch!" someone cried from the crowd. A sorcerer stood near the colossus, one of Korthos' famous lightning-strikers. A jet of white-blue energy sizzled and cracked, bursting from the sorcerer's hands into the colossus itself. The colossus punched, breaking apart the wall and sending bits of brick flying.

The crowd erupted into wild cheers. Some pumped their fists. "Hail Korthos!" they cried. "Hail Korthos!"

The colossus was a grand achievement, surely, but Thénai had done great things, too. They had founded colonies to match Korthos, but they had done much more—they had explored the sea, up until the wild ocean. They had written geography books of their travels—documented every tribe, nation, and people. Yet the Korthians wouldn't give them any credit.

He gazed at Theron. His face was emotionless as he beheld the colossus, whose hand had retreated into place after the stone-shattering punch. He had become a different person after Mount Hylea, and Phaido didn't like the person he had become. Once Theron had not taken everything so seriously. Once, emotion had touched him. Now, all he thought about was the task at hand, what the priestess on the Mount of Prophecy commanded.

CITY SQUARE, KORTHOS

The city of Korthos had stood for hundreds of years, Theron knew. Would it stand for many more? All the cities of Eloesus were old; it was said by ancient sages the Eloesians had been formed in this very earth and given life by the salty waters of the sea. Visions had assailed him at night, visions he could not and would not tell Phaido. He saw the cities burning, the men killed, and the women and children taken slave. And yet it was not by the hands of the trogs. Who was it? What was this "second doom" that Zoë—no, Io—had spoken of?

"Shall we go?" said Phaido with a hint of bitterness in his voice.

Theron had been lost in thought for weeks and it had clearly begun to wear on Phaido. And yet how could he not think, and ponder darkly of Eloesus' fate? Kronos—and this "second doom" had to be defeated. Why did it all rest on his shoulders? Why did he have to carry such responsibility? He did not even know if he was fit for the task.

"*Shall we?*" Phaido snapped, his bitterness clear and bold.

Theron grumbled something and urged his horse onward. He eyed the invention—the colossus—and wondered if it could be put to use. Surely it would cost him a thousand talents or more— more than the city of Thénai could pay. And what could a bronze war machine do in the face of such danger—in the face of a demon lord and his servants, and a second, greater doom?

The city square disappeared behind them and Theron followed the thoroughfare as it headed west and eventually became the Long Walls. These, they had built to protect Korthos' port, against the heavy protests of the Kersepolans. Thénai had long walls of its own. Yet in either case, Kersepoli had not prevailed. The most warlike of the states had the most pitiful of navies—it could not match the Korthians, let alone the Thenoans. Man does not live on the sea, the Kersepolans said, nor does he rule the world by boat—but the Thenoans gained their wealth by the sea, and spread its colonies across it "like frogs around a pond."

Like the road before, the Long Walls, too, fell away, revealing the bright blue sea underneath a clear sky. Hundreds of ships were docked here, unloading cargoes or preparing to ship off to Hymnia or to the Spice Islands, maybe Megaris or perhaps closer to home—*their* home. Thénai was impossibly far away.

Theron began asking around. One ship was headed to Thénai, another three to Tharta. One was headed to Hymnia and another to far-off Haroon. It was late in the day, after having asked many dozens of sailors, that Theron found a sailor making a journey to Tigris, the capital of the amazon queendom.

"Why are you going there?" he said.

"I could ask the same of you," said Theron.

"I will not take you except for ten *doukon* each."

"Twenty *doukon*," said Theron breathed. He had only nine left. "I can't afford it."

"Then you can't come," said the sailor.

"I can give you nine," Theron said, refusing to give up.

"I said twenty," the sailor said.

"Nine *doukon*," Phaido said, "and I will keep you entertained along the journey. I am an entertainer by profession… a singer, an actor, a lyrist by trade."

"A lyrist," said the sailor. "Where is your lyre, then?"

"I left it at home," said Phaido.

"At home," the sailor repeated. "Where is home?"

"We are from Thénai," said Theron. Honesty might not serve him well at this point, but it was the only way he knew how to operate. "We are exiles."

"Exiles!" Strangely, the sailor smiled. "Some of my crew are exiles. And you are in luck, singer… we have a spare lyre. We once had a musician on our crew, too… but he and ten others perished at a shipwreck… eaten by cyclops."

Theron knew the spare lyre wouldn't be at all comforting to Phaido.

"You may join our crew for the journey to Jogheira," said the sailor.

Theron emptied his coin purse, counting out the nine silver *doukon.*

"*The Trident* is a good ship," said the sailor, "and we are a good crew. I am a good captain… Gordios. A pleasure, I'm sure!"

THE KORTHIAN INLET

The wind caught in the sails of *The Trident*, propelling it outside its dock. The ship bobbed in the bright blue waters as Korthos and its long walls, its harbor, its colossus, its arrogance and its perfect white streets disappeared behind them. As Theron stood on the deck and savored the salty air, he realized he had never been on a ship before. It seemed impossible—Theron was a Thenoan. Thénai had by far the greatest navy in Eloesus. Sailing was in Theron's blood. Thénai had explored the whole of the Middle Sea; it had founded colonies along its rim, traveled from the isles of the amazons to the edge of the western ocean. Its geographers had mapped out the whole of the known world. And yet Theron had never been on a ship—never been on what had brought Thénai all its wealth. The sea was the second home of a Thenoan, and yet Theron had never experienced it.

"The winds are good. We may reach the first bend by nightfall," said Gordios. The fat sailor had a thick Megarine accent; he was a Ten Cities man, quite clearly. His crew, shouting and cursing, spoke in a mix of dialects. They formed a diverse group, a cross-section of Greater Eloesus. Perhaps they all had dark stories—tales of exile, theft and murder. If so, Theron and Phaido fit in well. What worse thing was there than to be an exile?

The olive groves and vineyards on the shore became high rocky hills covered in cypresses, and, late in the day, snow-capped peaks. The fair winds continued, speeding them along the churning waters. Theron began to feel sick—not for the sea, but for the uncertainty that lay ahead. Who would risk walking the roads of the amazon queendom? Who would risk visiting Tigris? Who would risk decapitation or grim execution—who, but Phillipidēs?

It did not matter what Zoë said. Theron was no Phillipidēs. He did not have hero's blood in his veins. He was not worthy to untie Phillipidēs' sandals, or even speak his name.

~

Night fell and the heat left the air, turning the winds biting cold. Some sailors were navigating by the light of the stars, while Gordios and the others—Theron included—had gathered on the deck to listen to Phaido. No doubt Theron's poor friend—used to rejection and small crowds—was nervous as he strummed the first few notes on the lyre. But then he surprised Theron with the quality of his voice, the quickness of his fingers and the choice of song.

He sang, to Theron's surprise, of Phillipidēs, who longed for nothing more than imperishable fame. He sang of Gaia, the mother of Phillipidēs, a pious and devout woman to whom Alabastros, king of the gods, had appeared in a dream. In that dream, Alabastros had made love to Gaia and that month, she—the Queen of Tharta—had found herself with child.

"Phillipidēs!" Phaido sang and strummed his lyre. "Phillipidēs! The son of god and man!"

He sang of the Megarine War, of King Sosimon and his love for Queen Prophylaia; of the hatred of Gaia and Phillipidēs' promise for vengeance. The thirty-thousand Eloesians had landed outside Megaris when Theron drifted to sleep.

~

He awoke at dawn to a view of snow-capped peaks, a cloudless sky and an increasingly choppy sea. He arose, cold and shivering. The sun would soon spread its warmth through the air, but the night's chill remained. Gordios was already up, giving directions to the crew as they scrambled about.

The ship was turning west. To Theron's left lay wild mountainous lands, rocky hills covered in cypress and cedar-covered slopes. Civilization had left them all behind. This ship, carrying countless amphorae of olive oil to sell in Tigris' markets, was far from any city or town. Much more travel, and a leg on the wilder open seas, awaited them before they reached the amazon capital.

A day passed, and then another. Soon they were on the wild open sea. Here, Eloesian sailors had traversed the world and planted cities like sewn crops. Here, they had made their wealth; opened trade routes with the west, brought in silks from Khazidea and spices from the Far South, aromatic woods and oils from far-off Kheroe. Here, on the wild open sea, they had traveled to the Blessed Isles and set up cities; they had learned the craft of sailing, and never been equaled.

Phaido had entertained them every night, and he and his voice had never sounded so good, nor had his fingers ever plucked the lyre so masterfully. Something had come over him; perhaps the desperation of the situation, the fear of the open water and the thought of shipwreck. Perhaps the gods had pitied them both, and filled Phaido with the talent and ability they had thus far denied him. He had sung more of Phillipidēs, of his exploits during the Megarine War—Phillipidēs, from whom Zoë had falsely claimed Theron's descent. What would Theron's mother and father say, god rest their souls? There was no god's blood running through his veins.

At noon, land appeared: tall palm trees on a flat, sandy

shore, and in the distance, the shady outlines of mountains. Had they truly reached Jogheira, the isle of the amazons? Phaido's gut twisted with fear at the thought. He was not prepared. He did not want to risk his life, not yet. The amazons' brutality was legendary. Zoë had surely been the kindest soul of them all, acting towards Phaido and Theron not with violence but instead only derision.

The winds picked up as the day wore on. The seas grew troubled. Rain began to pour as the port appeared. The rains and storms of winter were nearly upon them; soon the seas would be treacherous to navigate, and only the most foolish of sailors would ride the waters.

~

They docked in the amazon port. The city's buildings were white and flat-roofed, of a different style than the human lands just miles away.

"Goodbye," said Gordios. His men were already unloading amphora after amphora of olive oil in preparation to sell them in the amazons' market.

"Goodbye, Gordios," said Theron. "It was a pleasure."

He met Phaido at the off-ramp, and—unsteadily and unsurely—made his way to land.

PORT URSA, JOGHEIRA

How could Theron be so calm? He did not seem worried at all. Perhaps Phaido had been wrong; the blood of the hero Phillipidēs did, in fact, run through his veins. If the amazon kingdom did not frighten him, what would? Surely his mother had told him tales of their viciousness and brutality, their open hatred and their violence toward human men.

He could see them wandering the port—amazon women, some in leathers with glaives and chakrams at the ready, others with curved sabers clipped to their belts. It seemed even in their daily lives they had their weapons ready for battle. One he saw, dark-haired and dark-eyed, with a toddler by her side. The little one had a bow strapped to her back and a quiver full of arrows. No amazon men could be seen; Phaido had heard they stayed at home cooking, cleaning and taking care of the children. They had no chance against their wives, whom Phaido had heard were not only stronger but far wiser and more intelligent than they.

"Shall we go?" said Theron with baffling confidence.

"Why not," said Phaido.

Gordios led their horses out from under the deck. They seemed wild-eyed and a bit frightened from the long, dark journey, but calmed down considerably once on firm land and in the control of their masters. Phaido and Theron fastened on the saddles and then mounted their steeds. They rode them down the dock and onto the street. They did not evade the notice of the amazon women; some glared, while others merely looked away. Gordios was not the only human trader; others were unloading amphorae of wine and others of pungent fish sauce. Some were selling their wares here, in this grim port—colorfully woven rugs and tunics of fine Hymnian cloth. None would dare sell dresses or gowns for fear of offending the amazons.

They passed out of the town's stone walls via an open gate. A sign, pointing northwards, read both in amazonian and in Eloesian: "TO TIGRIS."

A country of palm trees and flowering bushes greeted them as a light rain trickled down. Another sign appeared in the same two tongues: "BEWARE, PANTHERS."

The air was sweet with the smell of flowers and the salt of the sea. Now Phaido could not bear the sight of the bushes and their bright red blossoms; who knew if a panther, sleek and black, hid within, ready to pounce and devour horse and man?

The dirt road led on and on; the ground ascended as snowcapped mountains appeared. The clouds dissipated and the rain stopped. The sun began to blaze upon the earth. They were in another world, a world Phaido wasn't sure he liked.

THE ROYAL ROAD, JOGHEIRA

There was something following them. Theron could sense it; he could sense it like he had all those weeks or months ago, when Zoë had stalked them. Yet Theron did not know the nature of the follower. Was it animal or man? Was it a panther hiding in the bushes, eager for flesh, or something far deadlier—a resident of Jogheira, an amazon in leathers carrying a glaive and a dozen chakrams? Theron did not want to frighten Phaido, but he readied his spear nonetheless, preparing himself mentally for battle if the time came. And the time would come; of that, he was sure.

"What's wrong?" asked Phaido, a note of worry in his voice.

"It's probably nothing," Theron lied. He eyed the flowering bushes, the towering palms which swayed in the winds, surely hiding a secret. He focused on one bush in particular, a thick verdant green, swaying unsteadily. Its red blossoms were the color of blood. There was a twang of a bowstring. Theron looked down; he had been struck. Stunned by the realization he fell from the saddle completely. Blood, as if following his sudden realization, began trickling down his side. He yanked the shaft out of his body and he screamed at the pain. Phaido fell flailing off his horse and hit the ground with a scream.

Theron raced to his feet and readied his spear even as blood poured from his side. He was as good as dead, it seemed, but he wouldn't let Death have him yet. He had things to do and a country to save—his own. He coughed and spat up blood. Dizzy and staggering he left the security of the road and hobbled ahead. Two men approached, unaware of him. They had dropped their bows and had drawn daggers, preparing to finish what they started. He did not recognize them, but these were Eloesians, not amazons.

Theron ran ahead and screamed wildly like a savage barbarian. He thrust hard as blood poured from his body, striking and impaling one man straight through. He yanked out the spear, sending flesh and hot blood into the air—the man's, and his own, and kicked the other to the ground. He pitched back his spear and prepared to arc it into the man's chest and end his wicked life.

"Mercy!" he cried. "Mercy!"

Theron stopped himself, forcing his mind to overcome his boiling rage. "Who are you?" he howled.

"Nikos of Thénai!"

The name was meaningless to him. "Who sent you?" Theron roared. The pouring blood had soaked into his pants and breeches. He was nearly gagging on the blood welling up in his mouth.

"Our archon… Epaphras!" he cried.

Epaphras. Why? It made no sense to Theron. Epaphras had made them exiles; was that not enough punishment? Was that not enough humiliation? Was that not considered, by the wider Thenoan community, to be worse than death? "Why?" howled Theron as his body weakened. He did not understand.

"I was a murderer, liable to be killed!" Nikos howled. "I wanted to save my own life! Epaphras promised me life, and coin!"

"Not you, scum!" Theron hissed. "Why does Epaphras want me dead?"

"I… I don't know. You are Theron, no?" Nikos was growing too comfortable now, too certain of Theron's mercy. "Epaphras has changed. He has become something else, someone different… someone frightening. He is strange. He has been changing… he has been growing h—"

Theron slammed his spear into the man's chest, who grunted like pig. His eyes widened and Theron stabbed him again.

Theron was going to die; of that, he was certain. He staggered toward the road, weakened, and found Phaido barely clinging to life. An arrow had pierced his friend in the chest. Theron wept at the thought of losing him. He grabbed Phaido and heaved him into his arms. He staggered down the road, weeping all the way, and made it not ten yards before he collapsed onto the hard dirt of the road.

THE HOUSE OF KORA, TIGRIS

Theron woke to a spoonful of hot vegetables, followed by a harsh liquid. Firewater, he recognized—the biting amazon drink legendary across the world. A woman sat before him, looming over him above his bed. She was dark of skin, much darker than Zoë but clearly an amazon. Her hair was bundled up into a tall ponytail—a shade of black with several strands of gray. She was an old amazon, an elderly woman clearly, but quite energetic. She had kind eyes that Theron would never associate with an amazon—kind eyes like a grandmother. Did the amazons really know of anything like grandmotherly love? It seemed so impossible. Theirs was a world of chakrams, glaives and sabers. Did they know anything of love and affection?

Appropriately, a spiked mace of iron dangled from the woman's belt. But those dark eyes were so kind, so loving. Were they really an amazon's?

"Who are you?" said Theron. At his words, the pain in his chest flared up. He fell into a coughing fit. Then the amazon woman touched him, and he calmed down instantly.

"Shhh," she said, "hush, little one. I am Kora, a Solarine."

"A Solarine," breathed Theron. The word was as foreign to him as any in the amazon language. "Where am I?"

"In Tigris," said Kora.

How could an amazon have eyes that kind? "You saved me," said Theron. "How?"

"I had been following you," said Kora. "I was told of your arrival by the Sun Goddess herself… or so it seems. I saw your arrival in a dream. You came from the Mount of Prophecy. Destiny is written all about you, young one. That much is clear. I am sad I did not find you before those bandits did."

It all came rushing back to Theron—the struggle on the road, the arrows. Phaido! "Phaido! Where is Phaido?" He sat up but Kora forced him gently down. "Where is Phaido?"

"Your friend?" said Kora. Her kind eyes turned sad. "He is at rest. He has been sent back with the first ship to Thénai. He will rest with his brothers. His ghost is gone; he is in the next world now, surely laughing and drinking wine amid the birds of paradise…"

"No! No!" Theron couldn't breathe. His eyes burst with tears and he began to sob. He fell into a coughing fit. With one hand, Kora pinned him down. He wept at the thought of losing his friend. They had been through so much together. Surely the gods would not be so cruel. He wept uncontrollably and Kora wiped the tears from his face. He had never known such pain, such sadness. He could not bear it. He could not go on.

"Shhh," said Kora, "hush, child."

He thought of when he first met Phaido. He had returned from Thénai's great war with Kersepoli, exhausted and remembering the faces of those he had killed. The war had been won, Theron had thought, but at what cost to his soul? In a tavern, drunk on wine, he had heard Phaido singing. He had thought, *This must be the worst singer I've ever heard.* He laughed despite his tears. He could not see through them. Kora had become a blur—it was just as well.

"Hush, child," Kora murmured. "Surely he is with the gods now, in paradise. Anyone who travels with a man like you must love the gods."

Why did this Kora have such a high opinion of him? After all, he had somehow let Phaido die. If Phaido had not followed him on this fool's quest, if he had stayed behind in Thenoa to tend flocks of sheep, he would not be dead. He would still be alive—artlessly strumming the lyre and singing poorly.

Kora was brushing his hair with her hand. She was an old woman, it was clear, but had all the strength of her youth. "Why did you come to Amazonia?" she said. "You have no doubt heard we are vicious and cruel."

Not now, Theron wanted to say. *Don't ask me questions when Phaido's death is so fresh.* "I had heard it," said Theron, "but then I found out otherwise." The memory of Zoë touched him deeply. In a way she had died too—she had become a different person. Perhaps she had ascended to immortality in her new form, but either way, it was a loss for Theron, a loss as permanent as Phaido. "Zoë," was all he could manage to say.

"Ah, you met one of our own," said Kora. "Strange that an amazon would ever befriend a human man, but stranger things have happened I suppose. The gods once walked the earth, it is said, and so have demons."

Theron wiped his tears. He looked into Kora's eyes. What knowledge hid behind those dark orbs? Surely, she was referencing the demon Kronos. She was referring to Abraxas' Mantle, the cloak of dark wool with the demon's-blood gem. "You know," he said.

"I am sure I do not know," Kora said. "You are a mystery to me. Destiny rides all about you, but you remain an enigma. Why did you come to Amazonia, to this dangerous place?"

"Dangerous," breathed Theron. "I am in danger?"

"Not while you are in my house," said Kora, "but amazons have certain beliefs about humans. They range from open scorn to eager calls for violence."

"I seek the amazon queen," said Theron.

Kora laughed.

"I need her help," Theron explained, and Kora laughed even more.

"The amazon queen would never breathe the same air as a

human man," Kora said. "You are far too bold. The amazon queen would consider it an insult if you looked at her. Her Majesty is set above all other amazons… compared to you she is a goddess in human form. You are an ant before other amazons, before *her*, you are the lowest creature imaginable… a worm wriggling in the dirt."

"So you say." Theron glared at Kora. He sat up, realizing his strength had returned. "How long have I been asleep?"

"Two weeks," Kora said.

"Two weeks!" Theron exclaimed. "Have I wasted that much time?"

"Your friend is likely buried already, with his fathers."

Theron glared at her for bringing up the topic again, for reminding him of the dear friend he had lost.

"It is by my help that you are alive," Kora said. "There have been strange folk skulking outside my house. They will not enter for fear of me. I have not left you all this time… my handmaids have prepared all your meals and healing brews."

"Strange folk," Theron repeated.

"Yes, strange folk," Kora said. "Strange folk that seek to do you harm. Human men, some of them—pretending to sell wares here. Even human men dressed as amazons… they'd be dead, if they weren't so convincing."

A coldness settled into Theron and his neck-hairs stood on end. Kora's house was dim lit. There were no windows in this room. For the first time, he picked up on the scent of herbs and the idle chatter of handmaids. This Kora woman was wealthy, highly respected and quite clearly powerful. She had said she was a Solarine—what was that?

"I would wager all my wealth that there is a bounty on your head," Kora said. "A bounty high enough that human men would risk dressing as amazons or pretend to be merchants."

"Epaphras," he muttered.

A handmaid appeared with a foul-smelling concoction, steaming in a bowl. "My lady?" she said. "The potion is ready."

"Our friend has awakened," Kora said.

"Oh." The handmaid disappeared as quickly as she had come.

"You ripped that arrow from your side." Kora smiled. "That is an amateur mistake. You should have left it in. And the arrowhead had been embedded deep in your flesh."

Theron lifted his shirt and eyed the wound. The area around looked seared. It had healed, though.

"Cauterization, as only a Solarine can manage," Kora said. "Now tell me… what is your name?"

"Theron."

"Theron, you will never get an audience with the queen." Kora's smile widened. "What shall you do now? Shall I send you back to Thénai?"

"I will have an audience with the queen, one way or another," Theron said. "Mark my words. You won't be able to stop me."

He moved off the bed and stood up unsteadily on his two feet. He almost fell, catching himself on the ground.

"I would not go outside if I were you."

Theron rose upright.

Kora was not smiling anymore. "The danger is grave. There are dark powers at work… powers you do not understand. I fear you have brought evil to Tigris. More reason for the queen not to be happy…"

"I was sent here to speak to the queen," Theron said. "I have no other goal but that. I will stop at nothing to accomplish it. Phaido would have wanted it that way."

"And who sent you on this fool's errand?" Kora said. "This mission that may cost you your life, if you manage to accomplish it? Queen Daphnë admits only amazons into her presence, and of those, only females. She will have your head chopped off, clean in two."

"Be it as it may, I will see her," Theron said. "I will see her even if it costs me my head. Who sent me, you ask. None but the best… the priestess of Mount Hylea. Io."

Kora gasped. A startled expression had overtaken her wizened face. "The Oracle?" she asked. "Surely, you are joking."

"I do not," answered Theron. "The… Oracle… is back on her Sacred Mountain. What's more, I brought her there."

"Io is a distant memory now… she has been gone for hundreds of years," Kora said. "You lie, boy."

"Don't you dare call me a liar," snapped Theron. "I know what I saw. I know who sent me. I am many things, but I am not a liar."

Kora stared at him seriously, pursing her lips.

Message taken.

"The priestess has returned," Kora said. "You do not lie, you say. So be it; I believe you. Such news will spread from here to Kalormenë, from Straiteira to Agathë. Some say she is mad, but the wise know better… She is a relic of the Old Dominion, such as we…"

"The Old Dominion," Theron repeated.

Kora frowned and a sadness touched her eyes. "A great nation and a great people. *From many, there is one.* They are but a memory now. Fire and water destroyed them. They had become proud.

"We amazons are creatures of that old world. Like that old world, we are passing away. Each generation grows smaller. Soon our people will be the least of all in the Middle Sea."

Theron touched Kora gently. She shirked away from him. Perhaps it was unclean, in her eyes, for a human man to touch amazonian skin. "You are declining, maybe," said Theron. "Your numbers are dwindling and so might be your strength… but you are strong yet, and you can do some good. The Mantle of Abraxas…"

Fury replaced sadness; she struck Theron with a punch swifter and more devastating than he thought possible. He went flying across the bed. Tears of pain welled in his eyes.

"I… I am sorry," Kora said. "That name… never say it. It cannot be spoken. The servant of the demon prince must not be remembered. His name was blotted out of all the histories. True, his legend lives on, or how else would I know the name? But that doesn't make it right to speak it…"

Theron was still clutching his throbbing jaw. Tears trickled down his cheek. Engulfed in fury he leapt at Kora; she caught his hands in her own. In a snap she could break his arms, but she didn't. "Your anger is good," said Kora. "You can use it to fuel your battles. But before me you are a mere ant. I have far greater strength."

Theron could not argue with that.

"You say the Mantle has resurfaced."

"In Thénai." Theron still wanted to land a solid punch across Kora's jaw—no matter that she looked old enough to be his grandmother. No human grandmother or grandfather had ever had such strength.

"Your human cities all blend together," Kora said. "I do not know Thénai from Thartica…"

Thartica was a region, not a city. Theron smiled at the mistake.

"With such a thing hovering over our heads we cannot waste any time," Kora said. "The Mantle is far more destructive than your puny human mind can imagine. I weep for all those in your city."

And so did Theron. Though they had abandoned him, so many good Thenoans remained, so many people he had loved. So many friends remained behind, so many people with good hearts. He wept anew for Phaido.

"You must stay here," Kora said. "My handmaids look harmless but they can easily fend off any human attacker…"

"I will come with you," Theron said. "By the goddess above, reigning in heaven, I will come with you!" Fury surged through him, blazing for all the wrongs heaped upon him—by god and man. He broke free of Kora's grip and pushed her back.

"So be it," Kora said, "if you wish to throw your life away."

~

Kora's handmaids prepared a litter lined with silk pillows and soft cloths, with a roof of oiled wool to keep out the sun and rain. They raised Theron and Kora up, together, and began their ambling journey down the stone roads, alleys and thoroughfares of Tigris.

"Is it true," asked Theron, "that there are no amazon men at all?" Everyone—buyers and sellers, priestesses and merchants, warriors and city guards, were women.

"Men in Tigris and Amazonia know their place," Kora said. "They are not to be seen and not to be heard. They are to perform their domestic duties and remain obedient to their wives. They may not leave the home without a female escort, nor without a very good reason."

Theron laughed lightly.

"Your society is very unusual to us," Kora said. "Some can't believe it that men can go outside and socialize freely with women…"

The sun blazed upon the flat-roofed buildings of Tigris.

Palm trees grew throughout the city and the salt smell of the air wafted about, though they were many miles from the sea. Many market squares dotted these winding streets, and Theron caught sight of a handful of human merchants. There was the smell of fish cooking and frying. The scent of pungent shellfish, too, was evident. No wine could be seen—no bottles in the hand nor in the merchant's stalls.

"No wine," said Theron. "Do you not love life?"

"A mouthful of firewater and you'll be staggering down the street," said Kora. "Wine is for weaklings, it is said; firewater cleanses and purges the soul."

Past the winding roads, through the baking hot streets, the handmaids carried the litter. The sky was bright blue, with only a few wispy clouds in the sky. The congested avenues opened up to a great town square, and towering above it was a white palace, ten times grander than the temple on Thénai's High City.

OUTSIDE THE QUEEN'S PALACE, TIGRIS

Panther statues of white marble guarded the palace, bringing—it was said—boons of protection to the queen and wards against evil spirits. Panthers and cats were the most beloved animals of Kora's people. Some amazons loved their cats more than their own husbands. Kora's cat, Jasmine, had passed on five years ago; out of respect for her memory, she had never adopted another. Her husband, now long dead, had been grieved sorely but only for a week. With Jasmine she had foresworn every pleasurable thing for a month, and then a year. That black cat with the golden eyes and the white spot on her neck had been her dearest companion.

What was she going to do with this foolish oaf next to her? As a Solarine she could sense the destiny which shone all about him. The goddess had favored this one; so much was clear. As a Solarine she could discern truth from falsehood; the Oracle had returned on Hylea's holy mount. What could all this mean? Queen Daphnë would let her in, but no human had been allowed in the presence of an amazon queen in recorded history. To let a human man inside the throne room, to view Her Majesty, was the ultimate unthinkable. Humans—theirs was a perverse culture, where men were warriors and bread-earners, and the women reared children. Was it any wonder why they were so violent, constantly at war with each other and with themselves? Was it any wonder they were so bitterly divided, so proud and competitive, so arrogant, so rude? Was it any wonder that—as any amazon sage could attest—the human race was doomed?

The handmaids lowered the litter down. "I must go," said Kora. She did not understand why she liked this Theron so much. Since girlhood, she had been taught to despise human men. Since she shot her first arrow at age three, a curse had been on her lips. Filthy humans, she had called them. Weaklings. But this one—not so much. He had a fire within him, and the destiny about him was almost visible to her old eyes—shining and golden, a halo and an outline of light, like the ancient heroes were said to have. Why did the gods favor him so? Was he one of them?

OUTSIDE THE QUEEN'S PALACE, TIGRIS

Theron watched as Kora left. The royal guards—women both, decked in suits of scale-mail with broad steel glaives—did not so much as sniff at her walking by. It was clear she was a woman of great respect, revered across Tigris. She was a Solarine—but what, exactly, was that?

The savage memory of Phaido returned. What had he ever done in his life to deserve such an end? What nefarious crime could he possibly have committed to deserve death? Some said the gods were always just, that everyone got exactly what they deserved—yet Phaido did not deserve it. Theron's eyes welled with tears at the thought of his terrible voice, his clumsy fingers on the lyre, the crowds he did not draw—the dreams that had been shattered by a single arrow to the heart.

People were lurking around the litter, standing off a few dozen yards away, but clearly visible thanks to the mostly-empty city square. There was a human man, a large bug-eyed creature with a bushy black beard. He was nervously patting a dagger against his pant-leg.

There was an amazon, it seemed at first, dressed in leathers, with a sword in her hand. But traces of afternoon shadow—brown whiskers growing on her face—made it clear this was an impostor.

How much had Epaphras placed on his head? For such thugs to follow him here and risk the wrath of the notoriously merciless amazons, it had to be an incomparable sum. Five hundred *doukon*? An entire talent, paid in gold? Perhaps he had offered a cozy position as a city official, a promise of no work and a generous stipend from Thénai's taxpayers?

Theron realized in a panicked moment he was not holding

his spear. Then he caught sight of it—it had been tucked under a pillow in the litter. Kora would never let him go outside unarmed. Every amazon, from age three to a hundred, had something sharp within arm's reach, and usually an arrow-stuffed quiver or an arm ringed with chakrams to boot. He grabbed the spear and left the security of the litter.

There were tall buildings surrounding the square, flat-roofed and many inhabited. Could someone—a great shot, the equal of the hero Teucer—let loose an arrow and strike Theron dead where he stood? Suddenly he felt less safe.

"I beg your pardon," said a handmaid. All four of them had remained behind. "Kora has forbidden you to leave the safety of the litter."

Theron would not heed the idle commands of handmaids, not even if they had the strength of a bull. These handmaids, each armed with daggers, might well be able to do him in—but they would never be able to tell him what to do.

The false amazon was approaching cautiously. The thug with the black beard remained still. Other shapes appeared—a few dozen human men, and more false amazons.

The handmaids drew their daggers. "See what we told you?" one said. "Fool! What do I expect of a man… a human one, at that!"

Yet the men never drew close—neither thugs nor false amazons. The Royal Guard stood watch close-by, glaives in hand, emotionless yet ready, in an instant, to strike.

It was an hour in the hot sun before Kora returned. How old she looked, how wrinkled and wizened, and yet she walked so energetically. Her face, however, was downcast.

"It is as I thought… Queen Daphnë will not see you," she

said. "She was offended at my question. 'A human,' she said. 'And a man at that!' It does not matter what I told her—that destiny is writ all about you, that you are favored of the gods…"

"Destiny?" Theron said. "You see destiny about me?"

Kora nodded.

It seemed so strange. True, Zoë had claimed—in her new, wild state as the priestess—that he had some relation to Phillipidēs, but did that have any grain of truth? Would she lie? "Destiny," Theron mumbled, "I have no destiny."

In an instant, Kora was upon him, grabbing him in her wrinkled hands. Her eyes blazed furiously. Something had come upon her. Her fingers were burning hot. Her face brightened to blazing white light. Zoë was staring at him—no, the oracle Io—inhabiting Kora's body, appearing to him. He could never forget those sightless white eyes which burned with madness and fury. A voice cried out from Io's lips—many voices, an infernal choir—"Courage, fool! Such passivity is beneath you! Reclaim what is yours, Hero! Reclaim what is yours, Phillipidēs… the world!"

The brilliant transformation was gone in an instant, replaced with Kora's sad, concerned, grandmotherly face. "Are you all right?" she asked tenderly.

At the words, Theron bristled. Channeling all his anger, he pushed her out of the way. He charged past the Royal Guards, sending them tripping out of the way. An alarm sounded and—heedless of the danger—he entered the Queen's Palace.

~

The Queen's Palace was a garden. Flowering bushes and vines, set amongst pillars and pools, filled this fundamentally outdoor space. It was filled with amazons—all women, having none of the seemingly invisible men—and the alarm soon sounded.

Theron readied for battle. His rage had died down. He tried and failed to put on the persona of Phillipidēs, but he could not manage. Fear replaced fury; panic replaced anger. The amazons were charging him, dozens with glaives.

One struck, trying to slash off his head. Theron batted the blow away with his spear.

Another struck, harder than before; again Theron batted it away, but the glaive was hooked and caught in the spear shaft; a twist and the spear splintered in two. "Phillipidēs!" he cried, but his supposed ancestor did not answer his call. He barreled ahead; a glaive nicked his arm and drew blood.

He ran through the palace of Tigris, shouting nonsense, putting on a big act—of a fearless warrior, but coming off as a livid madman. Some amazon handmaids ducked away; others drew daggers and joined the pursuit.

Theron followed a marble stair up into a white alabaster building festooned with statues and colonnades. The doorway fell behind him, revealing the amazon queen's own throne.

THE WHITE TIGER THRONE, QUEEN'S PALACE, TIGRIS

Such a throne Theron had not ever seen. He would imagine one in the cities of southron despots. It had to be sixty feet tall, with white tiger heads carved on the armrest. A towering staircase led to its apex, where Queen Daphnë sat.

The amazon queen was swarthy, with thick dark hair and bright brown eyes. A feather headdress, bright and colorful, made from parrots and other birds of paradise, was set—intermixed with gems—on her head. She wore no dress, but only a leather brassiere and a tight fitting loin cloth, leaving her belly and legs showing. In her left hand was a golden scepter, affixed with a bright blue sapphire; in her right, a broad-headed glaive. "What is the meaning of this?" cried Daphnë. "How can you dare stand before me, worm?"

Such a beauty Theron had never seen in Thénai or Eloesus; oh, to have her, to run his hands along that belly, to kiss those precious lips.

She left down the steps. "You do know the punishment for intrusion, don't you! You will be tossed from the rooftop and torn to bits by wild dogs. Or perhaps we can devise something worse for you… it is said the King of Fharas will lathe criminals in honey and let bugs peck them away, bit by bit."

But the King of Kings of Fharas was far away, out of sight and out of mind. The King of Kimgs had no interest in Eloesus, nor did Eloesus have any interest in him.

"Speak, pig!" Daphnë howled.

At that moment Theron was tackled, slammed into the

ground, into the hard marble floor.

"Unhand him!" Daphnë cried.

Theron stood up, nose bleeding, face throbbing in pain. He looked back to see all the amazons of the Queen's Palace behind him with glaives and daggers.

~

A long time passed before Daphnë had descended the stairs. Her dark eyes were glaring, yet strangely playful. "I told Kora you were not welcome," Daphnë said. "And yet you are here. You have chosen foolishness; it will end it death. But first you must tell me—why did you throw your life away?"

"Throw my life away," Theron repeated. "You don't have that power."

"Oh, but I do." The playfulness left Daphnë's eyes. "Restrain him!"

In a moment's span, Theron was restrained by a firm hand. "Whip him."

A whip lashed and cut him deep.

"Now do you see," Daphnë said, "what a mistake you made."

"I am not your enemy."

"True," Daphnë said. "The word 'enemy' has an air of respect to it. You are not my enemy; you are a criminal."

"A criminal." Theron repeated the words. His shirt had been split and blood dripped down his back; the whip had stung deep but he remained stoic and firm. "A criminal who dares enter your glorious presence. If your husband is jealous, let him come and fight me."

"Jealous!" Daphnë laughed. "I have many husbands and none are jealous. I would never take a human man as a lover."

"Many husbands?" Theron puzzled. He had heard of the Far South, of their barbaric customs of many wives, but of many husbands he had heard nothing. When he left the ship, docked in Port Ursa, he had stepped onto an alien land.

"Many husbands, yes," Daphnë said. "Five, in fact. I could afford far more, but five are enough for me. By them I have produced three fine daughters and a number of sons." A wry smile had formed on her lips. "Your name is Theron. Do you have any last words?"

"I come from the Mount of Prophecy, from the Oracle herself...."

Daphnë laughed. "The Mount of Prophecy. So, Kora told me. She should not believe any rabble off the street. *Kill him!*"

Amazon warriors sprang into action behind Theron. He turned and dodged their blows, remembering at that moment the gift Zoë—the Oracle—had given him. From his pocket he drew out the medallion; a slash of a glaive caused it to fall from his hand.

"Great Goddess!" cried Daphnë. "Stop!"

Theron clutched his wounded side.

~

The medallion's luminous gold had begun to take on a brilliant hue. Light was pulsing from it and the air in the throne room had gone still.

Daphnë grabbed the gleaming medallion and read the writing on the back. Its glowing gold shone bright on her dark and comely face. "I know this," she was saying, over and over again. "I know this. She did send you, she really did." She glared at the warriors behind Theron. "Leave us! And shut the door."

The warriors, the maidens and the Royal Guard filtered out. The door slammed shut behind them, leaving Daphnë and Theron alone in the spacious room. In the titanic shadow of the Tiger Throne, in the light of the glowing gold, Daphnë did the unthinkable—she embraced him. The medallion fell ringing from her hands. "She did send you," she said again. Their lips were within inches of each other. She backed away suddenly, evidently embarrassed. "You received it from her own hand. She has been gone for hundreds of years… she has not had power since the days of the Old Dominion. Her temple was razed to the ground by Abraxas' servants… in the days of Helēmon."

Theron wanted to kiss those lips, to run his hands along that body. He had been within inches of her. Was there a more beautiful woman in this world?

"Why have you come here?"

Daphnë's eyes were so dark and yet so luscious. Her skin was so smooth and soft. How lucky her husbands were to have her, even if they had to compete amongst themselves.

"Enough!" she howled. "I see the way you are looking at me. I have seen such a gaze before. It will never happen. I ask you again, why are you here?"

Theron fought the sting of rejection. Who could have her? Would any amazon man do? "I have come to ask for the amazons' aid… My friend died in our struggle." *Ah, Phaido.* Theron would never recover from his passing; he would mourn the singer and actor all the days of his life.

"Aid," Daphnë said. "Precious treasure?"

"No, precious blood."

"Will we send our daughters to die for the aid of man?"

Theron sighed, still hurt by Daphnë's words. "The Mantle of Abraxas… the archon of Thénai has it."

Daphnë gasped. "Thénai. I do not know one flea-bitten human settlement from the next. But he who wears the Mantle of Abraxas will be irreparably transformed. He will become evil and incredibly powerful… his soul will become linked with Kronos."

"Then you will help me," said Theron

Daphnë frowned. "We are not as strong as we once were… Even a hundred years ago we did not shy of war. I would not admit it to my people, but we could not win a war against you men; you have become far too numerous. Our number is shrinking. Our nation is shrinking. We are of another age… one day we will pass away."

"You don't have to pass away," said Theron. "You can still be strong. You can still fight for what's good. You can—"

"Enough," said Daphnë. The derision, the fear, the fire was gone, replaced with only sadness. "We will pass away as the Dominion has… theirs was sudden, ours is long. The time of Eloesus and of mankind has arrived. You must go, Theron, into the glorious dawn… you must fight alone."

"Alone, against a demon." Theron laughed. "You are turning your back on me… you are abandoning me."

"I am not abandoning you. I was never by your side. This struggle has nothing to do with the amazons. I cannot help you, and I will not."

Theron wanted to weep.

"I will give you safe passage to Thénai. That is the least that I can do."

Thénai—what else was there for him? What else remained? He could not bear the thought of the city's destruction. From there, all Eloesus would fall. *Two dooms,* he heard the Oracle's voice, *two dooms, and the second is greater than the first.*

This had all been a waste. He cursed at the amazon queen and spat at her. Then he turned and opened the door, running away.

~

Flanked by ten of Daphnë's Royal Guard on either side, Theron made his way across the island and into Port Ursa. He could barely bring himself to walk. He grieved not for Phaido anymore, nor for himself, but for Eloesus, the only home he had ever known. What terrible fate lay ahead of it—what turmoil? What destruction? When Theron was the only thing standing between Eloesus and utter destruction, they had no hope, no hope at all.

THE SEA

Amazon ships had many sails and many more rowers. The amazons, it seemed, did not keep slaves. Perhaps the amazon women thought it beneath their dignity to have people taking on the undesirable tasks. That, after all, was what husbands were for.

They were sailing in the cusp of winter, when the waters turned unnavigable even for the best Thenoan sailors. Soon waves would be crashing deep onto the shore, and rainstorms and thunderstorms would churn the seas.

He looked at the skies, at its many clouds, and the choppy seas beneath the deck. He thought of Phaido. He thought of his lyre, his voice, his terrible music. He raged at Daphnë, that because of her Phaido's death was in vain. The amazon queen had thought only of herself, of her own people.

Thunderheads were rolling in. The air began to smell of smoke. There was a lightning flash; it reminded him of the way the torchlight shone upon Daphnë's hair.

~

When the storm passed the next day, the shore appeared—endless hills, pastures and olive groves. The familiar sight of home did not comfort him; it only caused the worm of anxiety to creep through his belly. Things had changed; he could sense it from just looking. Things were different in Eloesus, and worse.

In the waning hours of the evening, as Theron ate a dinner of hard bread and harsh firewater, high mountains appeared, and the ship began to sail around the shore.

~

Winds carried them quickly the next day. The sky was clear and blue, but the air had grown crisp. Winter lurked just around the corner—a phantom that sought to strike.

In the twilight of that day a wonder appeared before them—a ship lying idle, burning in a great smoking inferno. Crates and barrels were floating in the water. One sailor was clinging to a barrel, his eyes wide, his lips trembling. He was muttering something—"*Turn back*," he mumbled, quiet at first, "Turn back!"

"Turn back!" he was screaming. "*Turn back!*"

The amazon ship passed him by.

Theron slept uneasily that night, trusting the amazons to sail by the light of the stars.

~

The day broke and another burning ship appeared. Theron was at a loss how it could have happened. "Eloesian fire," it was called, had been an invention of Korthian chemists, but no one would use it against merchant ships. Crates full of goods were floating around them. These were not ships of war. Besides, not even Kersepoli dared to attack Thénai for fear of a drawn-out war of attrition…

The amazon captain was shouting to her crew in her native tongue. Her brows were furrowed; worry was written all over her face. Theron hurried across the deck and asked what was wrong.

The amazon captain glared at him. "Don't worry, human. It's, ehrm, something in the water."

Theron rushed to the side of the boat and leaned over the railings. There were, indeed, strange shapes in the water—like squids, but larger, with bright red skin. Theron had never seen anything like them, nor heard of them.

Outside Thénai's harbor was something like a ship graveyard—the water was thick with rubble and driftwood, all of it burned to crisp. Other ships were still burning—several dozen—and crates and barrels floated everywhere. The contents of amphorae floated too—grain, olives, and other merchandise. None of this made sense.

When the amazons docked in the harbor, there were no attendants, no merchants or people from the wooden docks all the way to the start of the Long Walls. The naval registry, the offices and shops were all abandoned. Nothing stirred, not even a dog.

The amazon captain approached him. "We have arrived," she said. "Now leave us. This is an evil place."

They would leave him here, as typical amazon callousness demanded. He had no spear or sword, no shield, no armor. He was practically defenseless for whatever lay ahead. He left the safety of the ship and walked out on the harbor, toward the Long Walls. He hesitated before he reached the open gate. The amazon ship was leaving—its many sails were struggling in the unfavorable wind. It was stalling just outside the harbor. Something was happening.

A bright red blast broke the ship apart, a column of fire that instantly set its wood ablaze. Even here, Theron could hear their terrified screams. Unable to bear the sight, seized with panic, Theron ran from the Long Walls out through the harbor's gate, toward the wilderness. He was not fit for the task set before him. He was not fit for anything but running away.

~

The cold air was made colder by a blowing wind. Theron was not adequately prepared for winter. Where could he hide?

He gazed the city of Thénai and the red glow emanating from its hearth-fires. Why had the fire struck just when Theron left?

Why had all those amazons died? Somehow, he was responsible for it. Somehow, he could have stopped the massacre. If he hadn't embarked on this foolish quest, if Zoë—no, Io—had not filled his minds with grand delusions, those amazons would have lived. So, too, would Phaido have lived.

The harbor had been empty but many souls still clearly lived in Thénai. There was smoke coming from it, and the pungent smell of city living. Why had the harbor been abandoned? Was it being closed off? Had all ships been warned—"Beware, fire is coming from the heavens!" Had the strange fish in the water scared everyone off? This harbor-side road led to Thénai. He would never enter that city again. But the road would go on. Where would it take him? To barbaric Isteros?

His life was gone from him; he had nowhere to turn.

THE DEMIGOD

He faced his death with firm resolve
Without the Helm invuln'rable
"Now is your end!" the Mad King cried.
Thought he, "my own end lies at hand—
Yet I shall have this small reward."
Then answered great Phillipidēs,
"This is no end! I will live on.
Your name will surely be forgot,
And mine above all glorified…
Achieved, have I, what I long sought
The fame which does not ever fade,
The glory which shall never die."

—Arkelaios

THENOA

At the edge of the cypress trees, Theron was stopped by a cold wind. The rustling in the branches, the chirping of the night birds, formed a sylvan melody; but the wind stood out above all, cold, and refreshing. He knew that wind—he knew its name.

"Turn back," Io whispered in the wind, "or Eloesus will fall."

"I have no weapon," Theron said. "I have no spear and I have no shield. I have no hope of fighting Epaphras…"

"To the Lion's Gate," Io whispered, and the wind stopped.

Theron glanced back at Thénai, at the red glow of its hearth-fires. Night was falling deep over the land. There was a rumble of thunder. Rain began to pour. Theron bolted ahead, into the wilderness, caring not for his own life, nor for that of Eloesus.

~

The grass of the forest was bright gold, in sore need of winter rains. The leaves of the oaks and cypresses were rustling in the wind. Bandits hid in these woods, Theron knew, but what else but banditry could he hope for? As an exile he was even lower than a slave. He could hold no other profession besides robbing. *And all because of Phaido… and that damnable cloak.*

The wind was gusting, sending spattering rain dripping down Theron's already-filthy clothes. He dreamed of the hot baths he used to take in Thénai—a tub full of steaming-hot water; a hunk of lye soap. He thought of the wine and the good food he had eaten almost every meal—food that made the hard bread and firewater of the amazons seem inedible.

He took shelter underneath an oak, shivering in the cold.

Thunder cracked overhead; the hammer of the lightning god Arephon was striking the heavenly anvil. Theron had never felt so alone.

~

In the dark of night there was a loud crack of thunder and a blue flash of lightning. Theron awoke with a gasp. The light had outlined a figure standing just yards away, a woman. Her eyes were white and sightless. Another lightning strike confirmed what he thought; the body, nude save for a white cloth clutched in her hands—and a snake twined like wire around her leg.

Theron ran.

"Do not run, Phillipidēs!" Io cried. "Do not run from your destiny!"

~

As he ran through the forest, his mind was assailed with visions. Off beyond the trees, he could see the city of Thénai in flames. To his right were a thousand warriors in chainmail, bearing curved sabers of a strange make. Ahead, he could see his friends from Thénai, their necks bound with collars, whipped by a slave-master. "Enough!" Theron howled. He slumped to the wet grass and covered his eyes. Cold hands peeled them open. Io stood before him, her body shining with white light. She pointed ahead. In front of him was Phaido with despair on his face. He was wearing a burial shroud.

"Theron?" he said. "Will you truly let my death be in vain?"

Theron screamed at the Oracle's manipulation. He turned to her and saw that a sword was suddenly in his hand.

THE WOODS OF GYGES, HUNDREDS OF YEARS AGO

Who was this woman to tell Phillipidēs what to do? Phillipidēs, a member of a god-descended family? Phillipidēs, a Thartan of noble blood?

This blind madwoman was threatening him with all manner of hellfire and raining brimstone, but she could not back up her words with action. She stood there in the nude, among the oaks. The serpent twined around her ankle and leg, before emerging around her bosom in a green head. A woman so clothed was no less than a common prostitute, a streetwalker rather than a courtesan. A courtesan could sing and play the lyre, and hold her own in men's conversation; a madwoman so clothed, who let a poisonous viper twine around her—what worth was she?

He drew Pyrax, his ancient blade forged by the craft of the Old Dominion before it passed away. On his head was the Helm of Invulnerability, by which his precious life had been saved on countless occasions.

"The land is in peril, Phillipidēs!" the Oracle barked. Her white sightless eyes were filled with hate. Beyond those eyes was a soul which could snuff out the lives of men, which could destroy civilizations and massacre innocents without a moment's thought. In those eyes was nothing less than hell. "Only you can save it! Only you, Phillipidēs!" she continued her screed.

But was this land worth saving? Was going to war over a woman's kiss ever reasonable? Could fighting in such war ever give Phillipidēs what he desired above all—imperishable fame?

"Imperishable fame! You will have it! O savior of Eloesus,

you will have it!" the Oracle said. The she-wolf could read his thoughts. In a moment's span she was snarling, ready to pounce. "Obey me, wretch, or I will devour your flesh." She never remained still; her arms and legs were jerking in spasms.

"I will not be commanded by a madwoman!" Phillipidēs answered her.

"Then I shall kill you!" the Oracle howled.

Phillipidēs had never struck a woman before, but this "Oracle" had to be quieted somehow. Phillipidēs would send her to the grave. He charged and pitched back his sword.

His blow, strong enough to split her skull in two, was blocked by a shield unseen. The Oracle leapt forth and tackled him. Phillipidēs dropped his sword.

He did not feel the snake's bite, but he felt the poison burning through his veins. He was defeated. "I yield!" he cried. "I yield!"

THENOA, PRESENT

"I yield!" Theron repeated. "I yield!"

He was groveling before the Oracle's apparition.

"Then do your task!" she howled. "Do your task, puny worm! Do it, before I devour your flesh!"

Another strike of lightning illuminated the night; she was gone.

~

The walls of Thénai appeared in the light of a golden dawn. Theron had been cured of his insolence but not of his fear. He was unarmed and unarmored, completely unprepared for the task that had been given him.

THE LION'S GATE

The gate was open and the gatekeeper's post was empty. The sounds of the city were gone—no laughter, no music, no shouting. And yet Theron was not alone.

A woman stood there in a hooded gown, her face hidden. Theron walked up to her. She was carrying a cloth bundle.

"Who are you?" said Theron.

"My name does not matter. I am sent from the Mount of Prophecy," she said. She unfurled the cloth bundle, revealing a sword of white metal, straight-edged in the ancient style. So, too, was there a bronze helm, blue in color, the horsehair crest long gone from it. In an instant, Theron knew what they were; Pyrax, and the Helm of Invulnerability.

"Now I will be invincible," Theron said.

"Not at all," said the woman. "A strong head-on strike will still kill you." Theron still could not see her face. "Remove your dirty clothes."

"Will I fight in my underclothes?"

"Less."

Theron blushed. He knew of the sculptures of Phillipidēs which the folk of Thénai used to laugh at. Phillipidēs was so confident in his prowess that he fought protected by just his helmet, with only a cape to clothe him.

Embarrassed, Theron obliged. Once every last garment was gone, he realized he did not have a cape—but then he eyed the bundle of blue cloth.

First, he set the Helm of Invulnerability on his head. Then he took Pyrax in his hand.

The woman clasped the cape around him. "Go," she said, "save your city. The Oracle sends her best wishes."

She turned and left. It would be a long walk indeed before

she returned to where she had come from.

~

The familiar stone-paved streets of Thénai had been silent and grim when Theron first arrived, but as soon as he appeared, dressed in the scant garb of Phillipidēs, laughter quickly replaced it.

"Ha!" a little boy laughed. "Who is that, ma?"

"A crazy man," she replied, and led him away by the hand.

"He fancies himself some demigod!" cried a woman as Theron passed him by.

Flushed with shame, Theron walked on. He could see the High City a long way off. Clouds were swirling above it, red in color, from which gouts of flame would occasionally erupt.

The laughter and embarrassment pushed the fear away, but not for long.

~

At the stairway to the High City, another woman stood there, dressed in the same hooded blue robe as the attendant by the gate. She had a wooden shield in her hand. "Here you are, Theron… the shield, taken from Phillipidēs' grave."

The grave of Phillipidēs had been long lost to history, but not—apparently—to the Oracle, who saw and knew all.

Theron heaved it into his grip.

The mocking crowds had vanished behind him. The embarrassment at his nakedness had been replaced with fear. His gut twisted to knots as he climbed the first steps up to the High City.

~

With each step, the heat built up until it was searing in its intensity. The flaming clouds swirling in a vortex above threatened to spit fire and devour him; yet Theron kept walking, weighed down by the shield. He could turn back, but what shame would that be? He had gone this far. Death was one mistake away, but he had made his choice.

~

By the time he reached the top of the High City and the white buildings of the city below stretched far into the distance, Theron was dripping in sweat and panting. The heat, combined with the taxing climb, had sapped most of his energy. There was a reason most Thenoans had never climbed to the top of the High City and laid an offering to Amara the War Maiden.

And her temple was still there, gleaming white in marble. So, too, were the law-courts; but there was no smell of sacrificed bulls, nor the sounds of talking or frenzied hymns. It was silent and empty save for the crackling of the fire—and a man approaching.

And yet it was not a man. The creature walking up to him had a trident in its hand. On its back it wore the black cloak Theron had taken, clasped on the front with the demon's-blood gem. Epaphras, the shady archon, was gone, replaced with a chthonic demon of the subterranean world. His skin was green and his face was bony, with two jagged horns. Along his chin were more horns. His eyes were yellow and his tongue, which flitted from his mouth every once in a while, was forked like a snake's. A tail had begun to grow behind him, not much longer than Theron's forearm.

"Epaphras," Theron cried. Panic threatened to overtake him. He thought of fleeing but fear and indecision froze him in place.

"Epaphras the fool is gone," said the creature. His voice was loud and booming, shaking Theron's world. It seemed to come from all angles and from within Theron's mind. "I am here now… Kronos."

Kronos. The word seemed to shake the very earth. It was shouted in turn by the mountains far beyond Thénai, and by all the creatures and wyrms far below, beneath the earth. It was a name that sent people to madness, that broke their minds and shattered their world. It was a name that sent people to murder, to steal—to destroy everything they loved. It was a name that Theron could never forget.

"Kneel before me, worm," the demon's voice boomed from all corners and from within Theron's mind. "Grovel and lie prostrate. Accept your death… end your meaningless life. Hear my voice and be destroyed…"

Theron ran at him, shield raised up, sword pitched back.

The half-demon thrust his trident forward, hitting Theron's shield squarely. He pulled back and the wood of the shield came with it, breaking apart into a hundred pieces. Theron staggered and fell.

I can't do this, he thought. *I can't.*

The half-demon stabbed with his trident. Theron rolled away just barely. The metal pierced deep into the stone of the High City. Theron leapt to his feet and backed away, nearly falling over. He staggered backward as the half-demon pulled the trident from the stone, forming permanent cracks in the ground. In view of Amara's temple, he had never felt so alone. The gods and heaven were gone from the earth, replaced with fire and demons.

Theron backed away like a frightened sheep without a shepherd.

A wind blew, cold and piercing. It gusted and pushed

Theron and Kronos alike. He knew that wind; he knew its name. That was the wind of the Mount of Prophecy, sent by Io herself. It was the wind of the gods. "Go!" it howled. "Charge! You are stronger than him!"

Theron charged again.

The half-demon kicked and sent him flying. The Helm of Invulnerability went flying from Theron's head. He hit the stone hard, just barely managing to grasp Pyrax. The half-demon was charging, now, faster than before.

The wind had been knocked from Theron's lungs. He could scarcely breathe, let alone think. The cold gust from Hylea's frozen peak struck him again. The half-demon was within inches of him when he stood up, pitched back his sword, and thrust it forward.

The white blade pierced Kronos' bony flesh, but as soon as he pulled the sword from the wound, the damage had sealed up. Theron cried out as the sword turned hot. He almost dropped it. He could do nothing.

The blood-red gem that clasped together the Mantle pulsed with light. Theron struck it but the gem was as hard as a diamond.

"Theron!" a voice cried.

A third maiden had ascended the grueling steps of the High City. In her hand was a bucket, full of water.

"Here," she said, "the last of the stygian waters… the last of the land of Stygia which remains in this world…"

But Kronos slapped Theron with his trident and Theron went flying. He hit the ground hard again. Surely he had broken something, from this great fall or the one prior. His body ached and burned with pain. "I can't do it," he told himself. "I can't."

No wind blew, urging him on. No apparition of the Oracle appeared before him. No, what caused him to stand up despite his aching, swelling pain, was hatred for Epaphras—and the faint hope that he could take his revenge.

The maiden ran to him, splashing bits of water which seemed to glisten like crystal. Was this truly the water of Stygia, of the forgotten realm which had vanished into history?

Like a hero of old he dipped his sword within, lathing it with the viscous, sparkling water.

Kronos was charging him.

Theron did not call upon the gods or heaven, but from the strength within himself. He pitched back his sword and slashed— the blade cut off a piece of the bat-like Mantle. The cloth burned to ash before it hit the ground.

Again Theron dipped his sword deep into the stygian water; the sparkling liquid dripped from his blade as he pulled it from the bucket.

Kronos, having failed to strike him, charged once more. Theron could see death before him—but he could not let it happen. None would remember him for failure. If he fell now, he would never have the imperishable fame he sought. "Ai!" he howled. "Phillipidēs!"

Sword struck trident. The wooden shaft wobbled. Theron struck again but Kronos dodged the blow.

Theron dipped the sword once more in the water. Then he grabbed the bucket and threw the water at Kronos. Stunned, Kronos staggered backward. His skin was melting. Theron charged ahead. "Ai, Eloesus! Eloesus!" He struck hard; the stygian sword slammed against the red stone clasping the cloak. It broke into a dozen shards which fell in liquid form to the ground. The burning blood caught flame, sizzling and then flaming out.

Kronos fell dead, but by the time he had hit the ground he had become Epaphras—the sickly old archon who had exiled him. The black cloth of the Mantle had turned to charred ash.

The sun was breaking over the High City, piercing the

clouds. The air felt strangely warm.

It struck him then that Kronos had caused all those ships in the sea to burn; he had summoned columns of infernal fire. He had preserved Theron to slay one-on-one; he had thought there was no mortal who could match him.

It was not so.

~

Crowds met him at the High City—the same number as might come for a high holy day. Thousands and thousands came to greet Theron, so many people that he did not know. Yet they did not come to make sacrifices to Amara the War Maiden, or see her statue paraded about. They had come to see Theron—Theron, who just months ago had been exiled. Theron, who had saved the city. And yet terrible things lay ahead, for Thénai and Eloesus. *One doom has passed; a second will arise, greater than the first.*

The crowd lifted him up. "Theron!" they cried. "Theron!"

THE ASSEMBLY, THÉNAI

In Thénai's House of Assembly, a crowd had gathered to vote.

"The motion," a bearded attendant read from a scroll, "to name Theron son of Theon, of Potters' Street, the archon of Thénai and leader of her people."

~

Evening was breaking when the verdict was read.

"By a vote of the people," the bearded attendant said, "I name Theron the Archon of Thénai. May he lead her to prosperity and great prestige… may he distinguish her far above all other cities. Amara guide him!"

The thousands of Thenoans cheered again: "Theron! Theron! Theron!"

Is this the beginning? Theron asked himself quietly. *Or a terrible end?*

THÉNAI CENTRAL SQUARE

Now dressed in the official chiton of the archon, Thénai puzzled at what was to come. He had no business as an archon. Would he raise taxes? Lower them? One thing was for certain—everyone wanted his attention.

"Archon!" a woman said to him, approaching him as he walked down Thénai's stone-paved square. "There is a leak in my roof and my landlord won't fix it!"

"Talk to the Politarch of Justice!" Theron said.

A fat woman approached next. "My archon! My child is starving!"

She probably ate his food. "I am sorry—" Theron thought of bolting away. He did not want this. He did not want this anxiety or this position. Overhead, the skies were white. A rain began drizzling down. He passed the woman by.

Two men approached. They were gesturing at each other. "He stole from me ten *doukon!*"

"He's a liar!" said the other.

Theron began to run. This was not him; he was most comfortable in the field of battle, sword and shield in hand. Risking his life was easy; living this dreary one was too much. It did not matter his rich salary. No amount of money was worth this.

A dagger pierced him. Blood flowed from his chest, soaking his chiton with blood. The dagger pierced him again and again. He fainted before he saw his attacker.

THE HOUSE OF THE ARCHON

When Theron came to, he was in a dim lit room, swarmed with government officials in chitons. A physician was operating on him with surgeon's tools. "I have not seen anyone survive such wounds," he was muttering.

Theron cried out in pain as the physician pierced his skin with a lance. "Who?" Theron howled. "Who was it?"

The officials' faces were grave. One spoke, one whose name he vaguely recalled was Gyges.

"We detained him," Gyges said. "A little torture and he spilled all—he was sent by the King of Tharta to kill you, but he didn't know why…"

Tharta had sent all these assassins, not Kronos? By Amara, how could it be? Why would Tharta want Theron dead? Tharta, the greatest of Eloesian cities? If Eloesus was divided against each other, how could they possibly face the threats ahead?

But what threat? There was no threat. The first doom had passed—and there was no second. Gods damn the Oracle and her madness. Everything she had said was a lie. *Gods damn her. Gods damn them all…*

EPILOGUE

Amid the towering statues of Seshán, underneath the glaring sun, the warriors which the King of Kings had called forth began to filter in: tiger tamers from Saidoon, wild horsemen of Megiddo, armored warriors and bowmen from Greater Fharas, swordsmen of Zubay, war elephants from the lowland jungles, black-garbed zealots from Shakrath, and hosts of Shumahites and Korshahites, Ninshites and Alhambites, archers of Bajir and warriors of Rephah—a monstrous horde from the world over, a million strong, which would devour the land around them and drink rivers dry.

Before the titanic throne they gathered, parading in a hundred different colors—a thousand peoples gathered in his name. The King of Kings looked down upon the mighty host, by which he would subdue Eloesus, and stood up. Their roaring was like the crashing of the waves. Such a force none could ever resist. The proud Eloesians would fall prostrate before the King of Kings, and the whole world would call him god.

CONTINUED IN BOOK 2, 'A KING'S GAMBIT'

GLOSSARY

Thalos: A small silver coin, worth one-fourth a *doukos.* Plural *thalon.*

Doukos: The standard silver coin across Eloesus. It takes many forms but generally has the city's patron god cast onto the front and the victory laurel wreath on the back. Plural *doukon.* One *doukos* is about the daily wage of a skilled laborer.

Oros: A gold coin, worth fifty *doukon.* Plural *orhon.*

Talent: A unit of measurement, worth one-thousand *doukon.*

Agathë: An amazonian island northeast of Jogheira (see below).

Alabastros: The king of the gods in Eloesian myth. He is revered especially by the Thartans.

Amara: The goddess of motherly love in the Eloesian pantheon. In Thénai and the Amazonian Isles, she is also the goddess of wisdom and battle. Although a mother, she is a virgin. Eloesian legend states she is the daughter of Alabastros and the Earth. Her brother is Tyros, god of war.

Amazons, the: A race of people living in the coastal islands off the Eloesian shore. Their women are far stronger and—some argue—more intelligent than their men. Though they look similar, amazons cannot breed with humans. The child of an amazon and a human is always stillborn.

Arephon: The god of lightning, thunder, and storms. According to Eloesian legend, he is the son of Alabastros (see above) and the Sky. Hierophants are his priests. He is the most popular in the city-state of Korthos.

Arkadion: A village, the largest in the wilds of Themuria, called the Bride of the Wilderness. It is allied to Kersepoli.

Arkelaios: An epic poet, considered by some to be the national poet of Eloesus. He wrote a long epic poem about the Megarine War, a conflict between Megaris and its allied city-states (see

Ten Cities, below) and the greatest Eloesian power of the time, Tharta. Arkelaios hailed from Nautilos and was said to be a cripple.

Barbarian: A non-Eloesian. The Isteroi and the people of the Ten Cities are often considered barbarians.

Blessed Isles, the: A group of islands north of Eloesus. They enjoy a cool sea breeze and a mild climate.

Chiton: A knee-length sleeveless shirt, once popular across Eloesus but now restricted to priests and government officials.

Cyclops: One-eyed, cannibalistic giants native to Eloesus and its islands. Once widespread across Eloesus, they have mostly been exterminated throughout the mainland and now survive in isolated islands.

Eos: An amazonian word meaning "power."

Fharas: A vast empire, by far the strongest power in the world. It is ruled by the King of Kings, who is considered a living god. The word Fharas and Fharese also refers to a certain region and people—the heartland of the Empire where it began.

Firewater: An extremely strong, colorless and harsh alcoholic drink preferred by the amazons.

Haroon: The capital of Khazidea. It is famed for its onion-domed temples.

High city: A common feature of all Eloesian cities, a towering high ground—natural or man made—which serves as a fortress in times of trouble.

Hoplite: The traditional soldier in the Eloesian army. Each hoplite has a helmet and a breastplate, a spear and a shortsword, in addition to an iron-rimmed wooden shield. When fighting, he locks shields with his fellow hoplites, forming an impenetrable wall as long as he holds formation.

Hymnos: An island outside Eloesus, one of the so-called Blessed Isles, known for its black wool and textile workshops. Its largest town is Hesperios.

Ipsos: The second largest amazon town on the isle of Jogheira.

Isteroi: See Isteros.

Isteros: A region in the north of Eloesus, along the river Ister. The Isteroi speak a dialect of Eloesian but are thought to be outsiders, due to their pallid complexions and frequently red hair.

Jogheira: A large island of the coast of Eloesus, home to the Amazon Queen and the city of Tigris.

Kalormenë: The furthest amazonian island, west of Jogheira (see above).

Kersepoli: A large city, one of the four greatest in Eloesus. It is the most militaristic of the Eloesian cities and is ruled by two kings, either of whom may overrule the other.

Kersica: The region belonging to the city of Kersepoli.

Khazan: The river that runs through Khazidea, considered the longest river in the world. No one has found its source.

Khazidea: A kingdom far west of Eloesus, heavy under the influence of Fharas.

Korthos: A large city, one of the four greatest in Eloesus. It is ruled by an Assembly, elected by the people, and an archon, elected by the Assembly.

Korthica: The lands belonging to Korthos.

Laocon: A geographer from Nautilos who mapped Eloesus and much of the surrounding lands. He disappeared trying to find passage through the Sky Mountains.

Lion's Gate, the: The main gate of Thénai. Two lions are carved in stone above its giant double doors.

Long Walls, the: A series of stone walls which connect the harbor of Thénai to the city itself. They were built against the wishes of Kersepoli, who tried and failed to stop construction by force. Korthos also has Long Walls connecting its harbor.

Megaris: A city west of Eloesus in the region of Ten Cities (see below).

Megarine War, the: An ancient conflict, shrouded in myth and legend, between the cities of Tharta and Megaris. According to ancient tales, the king of Megaris Sosimon fell in love with Prophylaia, the queen of Tharta. Sosimon abducted Prophylaia and the king of Tharta declared war.

Megiddo: A vast plain to the east of Fharas, inhabited by tribes of horsemen. The plain is home to beasts of incredible size. Megiddi horses are considered among the hardiest in the world.

Mira: The goddess of light, especially sunlight. She is viewed as the creator of the sun by the amazons and especially the Solarine.

Nautilos: A city-state in the east of Eloesus, far removed from the ocean. Once great, its population has dwindled vastly and now it is more a village than a city.

Nix: The goddess of secrets and whispers, her followers call her the Gray Lady or the Queen of Sorcery. She presides over the knowledge of herbs—healing and poisonous—as well as hidden knowledge, wisdom, and the metals iron and silver. She is feared throughout Eloesus, though her name is invoked for protection from the unquiet dead. Korthos was historically the center of her worship. Her favored animals are the owl and the dog. According to Eloesian legend, she is the daughter of Tyros, god of war, and Seladora, goddess of nature. She was hated by her parents and cast out of the household.

Old Dominion, the: A legendary empire which was said to rule the entire world. It was destroyed suddenly, in one night, by fire and ash. Its cities sank into the sea.

Phillipidēs: An Eloesian legendary hero, the son of a Thartan noble who fought in the Megarine War. According to myth, he was given a magic helmet by the goddess Amara which made him invincible to mortal weapons.

Politarch: In the cities of Eloesus, these are the government officials answerable directly to the Assembly. They are charged with certain categories of oversight; thus one politarch might manage the food supply, the other the water. In Korthos and Thénai, they are appointed by the Assembly; in Kersepoli and Tharta they are appointed by kings. Their duties vary from one city to the other.

Rephah: A people of the Fharese central plain and heartland (*Gor Ilan*), descended from a warrior of the same name. The Rephathites are known for their tall stature and their warrior traditions.

Seshán: The ceremonial capital of Fharas. The King of Kings has his chief throne here, but the town is inhabited only by his hundreds of slaves and government officials. Great monuments and titanic statues dot its streets. Its most remarkable feature is the throne—a mountainous work of stone with steps leading up to the apex.

Shakrath: A land in the east of the Fharese Kingdom, a harsh semi-desert region. The chief town is Umron, where the Shakrathite king also lives.

Sky Mountains, the: By far the highest and most treacherous mountains in the known world, they block Eloesus from what lies east. Plagued by constant snows, deadly cold and frequent avalanches, no one has ever crossed them and returned.

Slavery: The institution is widespread in Fharas and offers slaves no rights whatsoever; they are viewed as objects or tools, not human beings. In Eloesus, the institution is banned altogether in Thénai and heavily regulated in Korthica and Thartica. Slaves have few rights in Kersepoli.

Solaricon: A disk, created in ancient days, said to contain the power of a dozen Solarine (see below). Containing sunlight in pure, refined form, it is said all creatures of evil and darkness are terrified of its light. The last of the *solaricons* were made in the time of the Old Dominion, before Eloesus was a state.

Solarine, the: In Amazonia, an order of warriors and magic weavers dedicated to the sun. Only women with magical talent may become Solarine. In addition to serving as religious leaders to the amazons, they have can summon gouts of bright flame— a flame so powerful it disintegrates everything it touches. They wear simple cloth robes and wield giant spiked clubs.

Sisterhood of the Sun: See Solarines.

Southern World, the: The non-Eloesian nations to the west and south.

Spice Islands: A chain of islands far west of Eloesus, known for its spices—chiefly saffron and coriander. They were once overrun by cyclops (see above) but Thartan settlers eradicated them from the region.

Straiteira: An amazonian island southwest of Jogheira (see above).

Stygian waters: Water from a lake in Thenoa (see above), which has long since dried up. The region was, in ancient days, called Stygia after the former city-state of Stygidos. A heavenly being was said to have died in the lake, imbuing the waters with its blood.

Ten Cities: A confederation of ten city-states, west from Eloesus across a desert, with Megaris as its head. The Ten Cities take great pride in their half-southron, half-Eloesian identity. They say they form a bridge between Fharese despotism and Eloesian democracy.

Tharta: A great city, considered the chief in Eloesus. It is ruled by a king but has certain limited forms of democracy.

Thartica: The lands belonging to Tharta. The region allows for extensive irrigation which results in plentiful food.

Thelos: A small town, nominally free but in practice, subject to Kersepoli. Once it was its own city-state, the fourth-most powerful, with its own port. It founded the colony of Hesperios in the Blessed Isles.

Thénai: A large city, one of the four greatest in Eloesus. It is ruled by an Assembly, elected by the people, and an archon, elected by the Assembly.

Thenoa: The lands belonging to Thénai.

Themuria: A region of Eloesus, wild and undeveloped. Being at a much higher altitude than the coast, snow is common in the winter. The region's chief town is Arkadion.

Theurge: Magicians who commune with heaven (white theurges) or hell (black theurges). They summon helpers, often called archons—not to be confused with a city leader—who do their bidding. Black theurgy has been punishable by death for many years.

Third Night: A feast day in summer, celebrating the dedication of the oracle's temple on Mount Hylea.

Tigris: The largest city of the Amazons, having about thirty thousand residents plus half as many slaves. It is located on the island of Jogheira. The amazon queen, Daphnë, rules from here.

Titan: A powerful kind of giant, present only in Themuria but once widespread in Eloesus.

Tyros: The god of war. He is revered in Kersepoli; yet he is viewed as never favoring one city over the other, delighting only in battle itself and spilled blood. According to Eloesian legend, he was the son of Alabastros and the Earth. His sister is Amara and his daughter is Nix, whom he hates.

Zubay: A group of islands in the South Seas region of Fharas. The informal, pejorative name for the Zubaydi is the Sea Raiders.

ABOUT THE AUTHOR

Cursed at birth with a wild imagination, Andrew Cooper spent his youth dreaming of worlds more exciting than Earth.

He is a graduate of the Odyssey Writing Workshop. His stories have appeared in Morpheus Tales, Fear and Trembling, Residential Aliens and Mindflights, among others.

CONTACT THE AUTHOR

Visit **www.aj-cooper.com** to sign up for the newsletter and stay up-to-date on new releases.

Find him on Facebook at:

www.facebook.com/AJCooperauthor